ANIMALS
IN
HEAVEN

(A family reading book for readers of all ages.)

BEN GARWOOD
Founder of Animal Angels Anonymous
Animal Spiritualist

CONTENTS

ACKNOWLEDGEMENTS

Peggy June Raccoon {Peggy Glavis Williamson] Wild and Wonderful Wildlife; Vernon L. Mink, Science of Spirituality, Davenport, IA. Elizabeth Korte, M.D., Macomb, IL. Otto Ohmart, Professor, Southeast Missouri State University, retired, Cape Girardeau, MO. Donald & Patti Farmer, Orlando, FL Pat Clankie, Office Manager, Rockford Public Schools, retired, Rockford, IL. Yufeng Wu & Jun Zhou, China-USA. Frederick H. Marler, D.D.S., Rockford, IL. Susan Roghair, President, Animal Rights Online, Tampa, FL. Clint Garwood, Public Relations & Marketing, Chicago, IL. Gayle {Educator} and Chad {Retailer} Farmer, Naperville, IL. Dwight {M.D.} and Marty Lindsey, Louisville, KY. Ginger Hepler, Child Care Director, Buehler YMCA, Palatine, IL. Michael Kotwas, Perfusionist, Chicago, IL. June [Nursing Education], Clayton {Chemical Engineer} Kootz, North Syracuse, NY. Randy Minnick, Pastor/Teacher, Porterville, CA. Becky Sanders, Event Coordinator Tarbutton Press, Portage, MI. Gale O'Bryant, Author, "Blackhorse Dances." Portage, MI. Cristina Lighthart Dyess, AR. Former Student, Author of Poetry. Samuel Martin, Spiritualist and Spirtual Counselor, deceased. Jan Woodard, Educator/Librarian, Jefferson, IN. Ryan McKellen, Cardinal Colorprint, Chicago, IL. Mark Huff, Rockford, IL. Lucille Vick Howell, deceased. Philip Ferrill, St. Louis, MO. Retired Union Representative, Communications Workers of America and Retired Telephone Technician, S.W. Bell Telephone co.

Cover Design by graphic artist Rebecca Shafer
cowham@earthlink.net Mattawan, MI

Baby raccoon (Sammy) compliments of Wild and Wonderful Wildlife
and his foster parents, Nancy and Dan.

FOREWORD
[originally written for]
What In Heaven's Name, ANIMALS?

Animal Rights imbues in you a sense of equivalence you can never quite shake. Enter grazing nature and you find a sense of calm and harmony you might not find in human society. It's obvious there is enlightenment to be gleaned from contemplating the contemplative beast.

Life, by definition, dies. Whether animals die as we do in full knowledge of its implications I do not pretend to know. What I do know, as I'm sure do you, is this: animals are capable of devotion and selflessness with regard to those they consider their charge. Indeed, one could be so bold as to call them as no less capable of nobility than we are, except that such a statement presumes they understand death the way we do.

Of course, death is the great problem. How do we resist!

How can animals regard death as we do when none of us seem to agree on this matter? Different faiths have completely different visions of an afterlife. There is no consensus.

Questions along these lines are speculative in my mind, but I enjoy mediating upon the Peaceable Kingdom, in which all of God's creatures live together in perfect sync. However, much as I have this Democratic Vision, I can see clearly the Law of the

Jungle is the way things are. Life can be very harsh with no mercy for the weak or the unlucky. Indeed, in my field, I must look into the incredible suffering animals undergo at the hands of humans precisely when I want to look away. Evidently Man is at odds with his fellow creatures. Unnecessarily he exploits them and is cavalier about the suffering he inflicts. Almost all of us are implicated. That microbes kill us seems only fair.

No matter one's faith, I believe Ben Garwood's mulling over the unknowable to be useful. Lively as it is, this disquisition is a summing up of the author of "Glory Bound." What I find bountiful in Ben is his resilience and wit. The grammatical and typographic quirks betray an American original. Spend time with the man and you can't help but emerge provoked.

Susan Roghair
President, Animal Rights Online
EnglandGal@aol.com

Animal Rights Online: www.geocities.comRainForest/1395

"Until he extends his circle of compassion to all living things,
man will not himself find peace."
Dr. Albert Schweitzer
It was also Dr. Schweitzer who spoke of the need to have an ethic
within our society that would include animals.

Animal Rights Online is an organization dedicated to helping the lives of animals. Every day animals are subjected to unnecessary laboratory experiments where they endure prolonged physical and psychological pain before they are terminated. Animals suffer for purposes of entertainment in rodeos and circuses, during the production of motion pictures, and in poorly designed zoos and aquariums.

Animals are subject to dismemberment and death in dogfights and cockfights. They are likewise subjected to 'factory farms' where their lives are spent in unnatural and confined quarters. They are slaughtered and their bodies butchered in assembly line fashion, then eaten. Animals fall victim to hunters and often suffer agonizing deaths in steel leg traps just so their skin and fur can be made into clothes. Often times they are drowned in underwater traps. Unwanted or abandoned animals often end up on laboratory tables.

HOW YOU CAN HELP

E-mail EnglandGal@aol.com Currently more than 5,000 individuals and organizations subscribe to the Animal Rights Online {free} e-mail newsletter. All animals deserve consideration for those things in their own best interest. Persons who could offer assistance usually have no clue as to what is taking place behind *closed doors* but through their newsletters **ARO** hopes to provide necessary education. Susan Roghair's mailing address is PO Box 7053, Tampa, FL 33673-7053.

Dedication

There are many persons who have been blessed with the presence of a single mentor during one phase of their lifetime, but few have experienced the treasure of more than one such person such as has been my privilege. Aside from my parents and teachers, my third and final (adult) mentor and best friend for nearly forty years, has been a man by the name of Fred Marler. Even after my decades of university education and the multiple degrees that followed, not to overlook class after class in the school of hard knocks, here is the man who finally opened the genuine doors of knowledge and enticed me to enter the bona fide classrooms of the real world. Although Fred had one of the best formal educations possible including the graduate school of Northwestern University, much if not most, of his education was self-attained. Fred has long been the most prolific reader I have ever known with a home library that boasts some 6500 carefully selected texts. Thomas Jefferson once said he could not live without his books, and surely Fred's books have been his umbilical cord to many of life's greatest blessings

It is a man with the intellectual wit of Mark Twain that I now introduce. An individual with the literary prose style of Hemingway, a man with an unquenchable thirst for what one might call *wisdom literature.* Here is a moralist with a philosophy comparable to that of Emerson who once wrote: "Nothing is at last sacred but the integrity of your own mind." Like Thoreau, Fred Marler recognizes each individual as a potential higher and independent power.

Fred possesses not only an encyclopedia of knowledge having to do with most any given subject, but a creative imagination so vivid, that in a heartbeat he can turn any otherwise boring topic into a drama so electrifying that even Melville would have found him a difficult contender of the ink and quill. Like Whitman, Fred revels in patriotism and love of country. His affection for poetry is second only to that of Frost. And what about his compassion for the lesser creatures mentioned in this book? (Scoot over, St. Francis.)

With a talent for transferring knowlege that my professors of higher learning could never have approached, Fred virtually resurrected men such as Confucius, Aesop, Socrates, Plato, Aristotle, Alexander the Great, Newton, Galileo, Michelangelo, Nostradamus, and Da Vinci as well as an endless list of others. He made history come alive with the wonders of their genius. Listening to Fred share the lives of such great persons, one could not help but feel as if he had known them personally and lived in their times.

This former air force captain and superb athlete was the man behind the mind who drained any notions of superstition, myth, or religious fallacies that might have once possessed me and replaced them with the influences of logic, philosophy, science, and truth. This is the man who enlightened me to that centuries old tragedy having to do with the warfare between Christendom and science and the gap of tolerance that even today divides one great religion from another. Fred Marler introduced me to the original seekers of truth. He gently brought me to the realization that even the greatest of minds are sometimes a little bit nuts, but that such individual irregularity does not necessarily take away from the genius they share with all mankind. Yes. There are mad scientists and nutty professors. There are whacko inventors and eccentric philosophers, but through Fred came the realization that it is important to realize even they have their voice and sometimes it is their discoveries that help to put the pieces of the greater puzzle together.

Never in my experience has there been a single individual that so totally encompassed the arts, the natural and physical sciences, philosophy, politics, religion, literature, and other convolutions of life's complexities. It was through my involvedness with Fred— the teachings and influence of this sharp-minded and wholly knowledgeable individual, that humanitarianism took on new meaning. To be a humanitarian can be as simple as sharing one's own gentle nature in the rendering of compassion and understanding to others.

During those many years aforementioned, Fred and his wife, Jeanne, along with Mary and me, would spend Saturday evenings together— enmeshed in our roundtable discussions. (We called the weekend sessions Saturday Night Live— and lively they were!)

During those earliest of years, Fred was also busying himself with the writing of novels and without my even realizing what was happening, Fred opened a new vista of interest for me in the world of the written word. Up until this time it had been the love of learning, but next came the love of writing. One manuscript led to another and then another.

Jesus Christ asked his disciples not to call him master, but rather call him teacher. So, to Fred Marler, I pass that *highest of titles* along and add another compliment by saying, if ever there was a man with a teacher's heart— it is you. Mucho gracious, Fred!

"Ben, it is an honor to have your book dedicated to me." Thank you,
Fred

Q

What must one do before taking another on a spiritual journey?

A

One must become the journey.

About This Author

Please allow this brief self-introduction of your author. The resume includes having been a public school educator for more than four decades; an advice columnist: *The Opinions of Price Rendelman*; a free lance author holding bachelor and master's degrees in education as well as decades of university studies beyond; years of experience in animal rehabilitation, founder and president of the national organization, Animal Angels Anonymous.

Perhaps an honorary Doctorate of Divinity degree, a document bearing this author's name, would be more impressive than the above credentials? There are those who would say such a certificate certainly would entitle someone to write a book about spirituality, and would it not? No. It ain't necessarily so, as the old song says! Know how that last degree was attained? It was purchased from a degree mill. You heard that right. Why? So as to cite an example of how easy it can be to misrepresent oneself when in truth such a person might be nothing less than a false prophet. There is a variety of such psychobabble on the market— all printed on impressionable scrolls with fancy seals, and for the right price— anyone can become an overnight pseudo-authority in just about anything. There are countless Bible-pounders and other powers to be with similar credentials to be found everywhere. Not to be surprised, for even during the Dark and Middle Ages, forged credentials were very common— noticeably so among the church leaders

Ben Garwood

and the ruling class.

"There are those who praise fakery beyond actual
accomplishment."
Aesop 6th c. B.C.
Aesop was one of the earliest persons to combine animal and
human spirituality.

Don't be misled, though. Although the availability
to purchase a wide variety of degrees with no
educational pre-requisite is as pitiable as an incurable
disease, the sincerity of this author's personal search
for spirituality is not. The many years gone by include
having been a member of several protestant church
groups including Pentecostal, Baptist, Methodist,
Presbyterian, Church of Christ and (presently) the
Worldwide Quaker Fellowship as well as Lutheran.
That exploration has also wandered through the
organized study programs of the Mormon, Jehovah's
Witnesses, and Catholic faiths including years of self-
study having to do with many of the other religions on
today's market, including several eastern religions
and a cult.

"God has many names although he is only one being."
Aristotle
•••

14

Author's biography by wife of 36 years:

This chalk-talker, as he describes himself, has rarely met a student or few other persons for that matter that he believed did not contained immeasurable self-worth. To Ben, everyone is filled with potential. People often ask him, "How can you put up with those kids?" to which he replies, *"The better question would be how can they put up with me?"* Even though many of his students came from backgrounds wherein they could not find substance enough to believe in themselves... Ben always believed in them. Whether in the classroom or without, Ben looked for ways to repair the defeatist attitude— to destroy the demons of self-destruction and replace academic decay with the love of learning.

To Ben, being a teacher is a calling parallel to that of a minister or a missionary. The educator's goal as he sees it, is to implant intellectual expansion, ethical transformation, and to modify attitude wherever necessary.

Ben holds fast to the belief that before teaching anything to anyone, the first goal must be to implant the desire to learn. In all his written inscriptions he attempts to teach. Exclusively he writes non-fiction and all his literary works strive for realism and observational precision. He does not believe the natural world as it is scientifically known to be all that exists. To explore the *yet-to-be,* seems to be his testimony of purpose.

The task of seeking answers to the question often asked of me: "Do animals go to heaven?" could not be shared by a more dedicated individual. Through his experiences as an animal rehabilitator, Ben has become thoroughly knowledgeable having to do with countless things pertaining to animals. For even more years than I have known him, he has been obsessed with the study of world religions and is as proficient with the diverse aspects of spirituality as any layperson could be expected to be. His dedication to research is inexhaustible and he consistently makes every effort to demonstrate expert fairness in presenting all sides of an issue. His writings are not intended to please, rather to educate and inform the reader, and he persists until he succeeds. For sure, he tells it as he sees it. He does not preach to the choir.

And now, back to Ben.

Charles Kingsley once said that except for a living man, there is nothing more wonderful than a book! A book can be a message to us from the dead or from human souls whom we have never seen who on little sheets of paper speak to, teach us, and vivify us. Their books open their hearts to us as brothers.

Q

How can one be sure they will always remain ignorant?

A

Don't ever study history or consider the other point of view.

About This Book

The search for truth is what this book represents and many inquiries having to do with both human and animal spirituality in addition to the big question as to whether or not animals go to heaven will be discussed within. Most persons rely on scripture to answer that often-asked wonderment about animals— so know this: To attempt to reach any conclusion by merely citing scripture would be as useless as trying to fly by flapping one's arms. Whether animals go to heaven is a deep and serious subject that deserves an inclusive and well-researched answer.

Animals In Heaven is intended to be educationally informative as well as reader friendly and entertaining. In spite of this author's best efforts to provide proof positive for all topics discussed, many questions presented within fall into the category of the science of the unknown and some queries simply cannot be answered. Although various philosophies, i.e., values, beliefs, and viewpoints will be shared— there is no

17

proselytizing to be found.

Among the topics included between these covers: Is there such a thing as psychic phenomenon? What is reincarnation? Does the soul evolve? Can people really talk to animals? Can animals talk to people? What was human life like— hundreds or even thousands of years past? Is anything material or does everything exist only in the mind of God and if so do we therefore live in a state of virtual reality? Can a physical body exist without organs? Do human beings have more than five senses? Wouldn't it be sad if your pet went to heaven and you didn't?

Some might believe it to be a peculiarly bizarre approach to include animal and human spirituality in the same breath, but how better to determine if animals can go to heaven then by asking and answering those related questions? And if a valid and intelligent response is to be provided— those premises and all others from which a truth is inferred ought to be considered. We must validate the postulates— the assumptions. This book is not intended to add startling new revelations to those who consider themselves to be among the intelligentsia. It is not about braininess or high-level thinking. *Animals In Heaven* does not require the reader to be quick of mind or clever. Instead it is a book for the common, not-so-highbrow person who might enjoy some optimistic reading having to do with a collection of many interesting wonderments.

Like my book about human and animal spirituality titled *The Search for Truth*, this book is also about the search for truth! If there is one thing all of us should treasure in this life, it is truth. Some persons fear the truth. They hide from truth. See no evil, hear no evil, speak no evil. Translated that means, see no truth— hear no truth— speak no truth.

The Truth, the whole truth, and nothing but the truth.
Sworn oath used in courtrooms.

Prologue, Preamble & Opening Remarks

When I was twelve years old, I met a very old man from the mountains. He became one of the best friends I ever had. Once he said to me, "The greatest tragedy of all would be to come to the end of this journey and have it revealed that we spent the whole time believing the wrong things."

Of course no one knows what they don't know. Think about that. Sometimes people truly believe something— but what they truly believe is not always the truth. Sometimes people want to believe something so much— that as that man named Aesop once said, they grasp at the shadows and miss the substance that is casting the shadow.

Sometimes students will sit in classrooms nodding their heads up and down in agreement with every word the teacher is saying. They are agreeing because they think it is their mission to agree. Recently a book was written that was titled, *Lies My Teacher Told Me.* Now it is not likely that many teachers would deliberately lie to their students— but what if the teacher was misinformed? Persons sitting in church congregations often nod their heads up and down when listening to their ministers, and similar behavior takes place when politicians make speeches. Are these persons really thinking for themselves— or could they be robotic followers? Do they agree just because they're *members of the* club?

Sometimes it is almost as if they have been or are being hypnotized. Maybe they're simply not listening to what is really being said rather blindly endorsing what they hope is being said.

Many of the students who have sat in my classrooms over the years have been excellent thinkers. An individual by the name of Mark Huff, who was a seventh grader at the time, once handed me something he had written:

> "Trying to soar but don't know where to go. Here or there... what if I don't fit in anywhere? What I do know is wherever I go my beliefs will always be with me. So in what way shall I turn? Which way shall I choose to my new path?"

Have you ever heard someone say, "Today is the first day of the rest of your life?" That is sort of what Mark was saying when he talked about choosing his new path. He is a very perceptive young man that thinks ahead... imagining about that journey to come... a voyage that will become the rest of his life.

The name of the aforementioned mountain man was Samuel Martin. Sam could best be described as an extraordinarily self-educated philosopher. Old Sam always said that no matter where we're going, we'd best have a map. A plan. Now there are all kinds of maps, but the diagram Sam was talking about wasn't one that could be found printed on paper but a chart that might only be found in one's head. You might call it— a *system of ideas.* Your blueprint of what the world is about and how you will fit into it. Such a schematic could even be you asking, "Who" am I and "where" am I going? "Why" do I want to go there and "how" will I get there?

Now here's a good question. When one speaks of a journey— is that journey to be restricted to (just) this life or what happens after this life as well? That's another thing this book will chat about... the possibility of an *afterlife*— not only for our own kind, but an afterlife for animals as well.

Of course there are those people who say animals don't have an existence after this one. With all respect, I say they are wrong and this book will reflect the claims that support that reasoning.

> "From such crooked wood as that which man is made of, nothing straight can be fashioned."
> **Kant**

Although having had a lifelong interest in animal spirituality, it was a series of experiences following the publication of my wife's book, *Pawprints Upon My Heart* that contributed to this interest having to do with writing about the afterlife of animals. Mary's book was published by Tarbutton Press, with the foreword written by the distinguished Timothy M. O'Brien, President of the American Humane Association. Not long after the book was released, Mary was inundated with the question from countless of her readers: "Do animals go to heaven?"

Admittedly, she realized that neither she nor anyone else could claim divine expertise in providing such an answer. Nonetheless she began to search for whatever proper answers might constitute a somewhat intellectual, emotional, and spiritual journey into that wondering of the unknowable.

Mary is a very interesting person. We first met nearly forty years ago when I was a water-safety instructor and the manager of a swim club. Mary had signed-up for one of my classes that would qualify her to become a lifeguard. Soon came the realization that not only was Mary an outstanding athlete, she was also a unique person in many other ways. We not only shared an enthusiasm for water activities, but among other things we found a common interest for nature, music, reading, and the love of animals.

After we married, it seemed that much of Mary's time was spent changing diapers, preparing formulas and trying to balance her college classes. Even so, she managed to operate her own private music studio out of our home. As if she didn't have enough to do, one of her piano students came to his lesson with an injured bird. Mary agreed to care for the bird and soon restored it to its physically fit, former self. Then came another bird and yet another. Soon Mary was known as the "The Bird Lady" among the neighborhood children.

During that year, we became very close friends with a veterinarian. Upon observing Mary's uncanny ability to care for the injured birds, he began bringing her many other injured and orphaned wildlife creatures that had been brought to his animal hospital. Soon it was a raccoon here— an opossum there. That was many years ago, but even now as licensed animal rehabilitators, Mary and I care for animals in need.

Also due to the influential and philosophical mentoring from the man to whom this book is dedicated, Mary has since become the author of children's stories and animal books. She smiles modestly when hearing her unofficial title as *America's Favorite Animal Angel,* and quickly assures those who are praising her that there are countless animal angels who are all deserving of the same or a similar title.

As Mary, an animal advocate in the fullest sense of the word, began to ponder just how to respond to the question, *"Do animals go to heaven,"* this somewhat snoopy husband of hers asked where she expected to find reputable answers. "Well, hopefully in the gospel," she replied. Shortly thereafter she handed me her notes and said, "You're practically a walking encyclopedia— and you've studied religion all your life— why don't you write this one?" But wait— had I not once— years ago drafted page after page of manuscript material dealing with that very subject and laid it aside? For sure, and therefore an extensive amount of research was already within reach.

There was something else worth mentioning that was stashed-away with that forgotten manuscript...thousands of favorite quotations that had been collected and indexed since middle school. That particular fascination was a hobby both my father and I pursued until it had become an obsession in years past. Dad once planned to compile an anthology of sayings, quotes, aphorisms, adages, proverbs, and maxims for publication. That never materialized, but my classroom walls and bulletin boards have long since been plastered with those morsels of wisdom, mostly from pre-twentieth century contributors. Sharing the mind of persons from centuries past when teaching things historical has always been a valuable classroom tool and how useful their perceptions would now become!

[Credit will be given to the source when quotes come from a known originator. When the origin of a quote is not known, only the quote will appear.]

Do animals go to heaven?

A

Does a bear poop in the woods?

SOURCES

While digging through hundreds of books and compiling thousands of manuscript pages of information for the book *What In Heaven's Name, ANIMALS?* friends would curiously look over my shoulder and ask, "Where do you find all that stuff?"

Good question. For sure let's rule out formal education, but not because such a pursuit would fail to represent a credible source or a commendable goal. Rather that irrefutable testimony can also be located aside from college professors, their classrooms, and thought-to-be updated textbooks. There remains the option of pursuing that old-fashioned school of what is commonly called self-education.

Aside from the curriculums offered through the institutions of higher learning, much of my knowledge came from having been embedded in decades of studies from the genius of men like A.D. White, Ezra Cornell, and Will Durant, just to name a threesome. Those lifetime works of those men and others like them provided a step-by-step search that led to what became a foundation of factual information having to do with religion, history, and philosophy of centuries gone by.

Beyond any original source, a cross-referencing of all details is a must. Even when dealing with a single topic, it is imperative to blend the perspectives and findings of as many historians as possible. When it comes to reading about the history of centuries past, rarely was a first-person historian or author present, so we might be required to rely upon the sometimes piecemeal transcripts of hand-me-down tales. Information might therefore be gleaned from legions of sources— some reliable and (apologetically) some not.

> "Without the dependability of the written word found in books, from what other source could we even begin our search for ancient truth?"

When seeking data having to do with religion, a choice starting place for me is my own religious library inherited from a former friend who was a retired Lutheran pastor. The hundreds of books therein (some ancient) now represent decades of concentrated study and acquired knowledge. Another of my hobbies through the years was to search for out-of-publication sets of encyclopedias and out of print history books. Those first such books and thus the igniter of that interest, came from the personal library of my father (1901-1994) who was an avid student of history. As much as possible, I find much value in referring to old books from the 1800's.

One curious onlooker asked, *"*How many sources did you use?*"* Well, for *What In Heaven's Name, Animals,* and *In Search of Truth,* bits and pieces from about four hundred begetters, many out of print, not to mention numerous notes and articles along with many inestimable contributions from friends or those strangers such as Plain Jane who just happened along. Yet, history according to one source is not

Ben Garwood

always the same history according to another and the more times it is told, the greater the risk of varying interpretations and personal influences. That jeopardy however is offset by the greater likelihood of truth confirmations that result from multiple sources.

"The most important thing for a fact-finder to do is face the fact that without the facts there are no facts."
Samuel Martin

RAINBOW PARADISE

There is said to be a place of "life after life," presently known to no more than a few, believed to be located someplace between heaven and earth. Although none who have been there ever returned to bear witness of this paradise, legend describes it as the Shangri-la of Elysian Fields *resurrected*. It is said to represent all the glories of God brought together in one place, and that no words uttered could possibly characterize this abode of light for animals deceased. Could such a place really exist? Well, what if?

Although it dazzles with elegance comparable only to jewels, pearls, and gems, it is set in the quietude of both visible and invisible radiance. There are picturesque mountains extending to the stars. These peaks having risen from pre-civilized forested nature lands are set in an elegant primitiveness of fauna and flora and where only the trees of life have been planted. Meadows and fields are ablaze with golden flowing wheat while pastures of grasslands cradle mirror-like ponds and snuggle against the river's banks.

Not only does the leopard, wolf, lion, and lamb stretch out and doze together in the sun, but a zoological garden of every known genre of animal inhabits and roams this unimaginable state of nature.

"Eye has not seen, nor ear heard, nor have entered into the hearts of man those things that God hath prepared..."
1 Corinthians

29

Is this but a child's imaginative falsehood, this kingdom where nothing experiences death nor fears harm from another? How is it that here, the grace of God, gives birth to new meaning? How can there possibly be such a place— a world wherein the beasts experience the soul of their *otherness* and where the torn heart is forever mended? Is this but a fantasy of the bubbling spirit? No. This is Rainbow Paradise— a heaven/haven for animals. It is the very heart of faith— a treasure house of fantasies— a fairyland for those creatures that might have been *motherless* or had no voice.

"The greatest man is he who does not lose his child's heart."
Mencius

For those who can focus on imagination, there is a bridge of light that crosses the river of life and extends into another place known only at this time as heaven. Upon the arches of this golden bridge, that is said to be as beautiful as a rainbow, are legions of angels attired in silk-like raiment. These are the chosen ones— heaven's finest who have been selected to be with the animals in time-everlasting. Every animal upon reaching its endtime was brought to this new age paradise of exquisite elegance upon the wings of those angels. It is by that same magic that one day those animals that did experience the warmth and love of a human counterpart will be reunited with those persons at this *rainbow bridge*

"There will be no more death or mourning or crying or pain, for the old order of things will have passed away..."
Revelation 21:4

Animals in Heaven

"Sister... Sister, is that you?" The big brown eyes welled with tears.

"Brother?"

"Oh Sister. How long I have waited since that day we were parted. Tell me Sister, what was your journey like?"

"Oh Brother... it was terrible. The little girl who seemed so happy to be bringing me home soon lost interest in me. She neglected to feed me or change my water bowl, and although I was first brought into a beautiful house, I was soon thereafter confined to a chain with no shelter or shade and all but forgotten. It seemed everything I had done was wrong, and after awhile the only name I knew to respond to was Bad Dog."

"Oh Sister, I am so sorry. My journey was a beautiful one. The little boy would play ball with me and I would run alongside his bicycle. Sometimes we would roam through the woods and play by the creek's moss covered rocks. We would watch the fish swim and scurry from the frogs that would splash into the water while big lazy turtles would sun on nearby logs. The little girl would dress me up in her doll clothes and teach me to do silly tricks so she could show me off to her friends. At night I slept by her feet at the foot of her bed. I am so sorry, Sister, that your journey was not as wondrous as mine. You were the beautiful one— the first chosen, and when they named you "Cookie" before even taking you from the cage, I thought you would be loved for the rest of your life."

31

"No Brother, it was not so. I was swatted and kicked and once when trying to run away I was struck by a vehicle and suffered a broken leg that was never attended to. That is why I limp even to this day."

"But Sister, have you not noticed? You limp no more, and Sister, soon the angels will bring the little girl and the little boy who loved me so much and have long since grown-up, to the bridge just beyond the ridge. There is to come a time when I will be reunited with them again. And Sister, can you remember how those children who were holding me pleaded with the family that chose you that they might be allowed to have both of us? They so wished we would not have to be separated and that each of them could have a puppy just to call their own. Well now it will be so."

And at that very moment, an *angel of light* appeared and said, "Dismiss your memories of the past and come with me, for there is one who has just arrived at the Rainbow Bridge who is looking for both of you."

"In the name of the Father, the Son, and the Holy Ghost."
Scripture
"In the name of the bee, the butterfly, and the breeze."
Emily Dickinson

Yes, Amanda.
Animals Do Go To Heaven

ONCE UPON A TIME, a very important religious man was asked the question, "What does love look like?"

"What does love look like?" he asked. He replied that love has hands to help others and feet to hasten to the poor and needy. He said love has eyes to see misery and want. It has the ears to hear the sighs and sorrows of men. That, he said, is what love looks like.

This man's name was Augustine. He was born 354 years after the death of Christ and became one of the greatest, all time, leaders of the early Christian church.

How about you, Amanda? Do you have hands to help others? Whether they are animals or people, do you ever pay any attention to the sighs of those who came into this world less fortunate than you?

There is a word for persons who give unselfishly of themselves. Such individuals are known to be altruistic. They are very unselfish— thoughtful, considerate, kind and generous. Such persons truly believe it is better to give than to receive and they do unto others as they would have others do unto them. Through one selfless and philanthropic act after another, these individuals give to the world those things necessary to meet the needs of the disadvantaged amongst them and they know the "needy" might be found in both human and animal form. Such persons are the true heroes of this life.

Jesus Christ was one such individual. His followers, known as disciples, thought so much of Jesus that they began calling him, "Master." One day Jesus interrupted and asked, "Why do you call me 'Master?' There is but one Master and that is God." He then instructed them to call him, "Teacher."

What a wonderful title! What greater honor could any of us have than to carry a title that suggests we can share knowledge with another?

To me, when Jesus called himself a *teacher*, that made him even more special than he already was. Perhaps that is because I have been a teacher for nearly a half century? But teachers are like doctors. They cannot do more for the patient than the patient is willing to do for himself or herself. As one ancient Chinese proverb says, "Teachers open the door, but you just enter by yourself."

Among other things that Jesus taught— were values. One of those principles had to do with treating others as we would wish to be treated by them were our stations in life reversed. Here is how one Bible translation quotes Jesus:

"What you would shun to suffer, do not make others suffer."
Jesus Christ

Although religions vary in their specific beliefs, and although they might have different founders, there are many similarities between some of them. Consider these quotes from other *spiritual teachers* having to do with the respect and consideration we should offer others.

"This is the sum of duty; do naught to others which if done to thee would cause thee pain."
Mahabharata

"Consider others as yourself."
Buddha

What does the word "others" refer to? Would if be *just* people. Would it matter how we treated our pets or the animals of the wild as long as we treated people with consideration? What do you suppose Jesus or those other religious leaders would say if you asked them that question? That is an often-asked question, and here are some more replies offered by some great and famous men.

"The love for all living creatures is the most notable attribute of men."
Charles Darwin

"I hold that the more helpless a creature, the more it is entitled protection by man from the cruelties of men."
Gandhi

"We can judge the heart of man by his treatment of the animals."
Emanuel Kant

So where do you fit in, Amanda? How might we measure your values when it comes to the so-called, less fortunate beasts? Do you help to care for the animals in your house? Do you think to remind your mother that the outside animals might be desperate for water during dry spells? That is especially true of the ground animals such as squirrels, raccoons, rabbits, and chipmunks.

Proverbs (12:10) says that a righteous man regardeth the life of his beast: but the tender mercies of the wicked are cruel." Tender mercies, of course, would be defined as a lack of consideration. The Koran, which is the Islamic sacred book believed by those followers to be the sacred word of God, says that there is not an animal on the earth nor a flying creature on two wings that are not people unto you.

> "A good deed done to an animal is as meritorious
> as a good deed done to a human being,
> while an act of cruelty to an animal is as bad
> as an act of cruelty to a human being."
> **Mohammed**

There is no end to the directions having to do with the treatment of animals:

> "Any interference with the body of a live animal which causes
> pain or
> disfigurement is contrary to the Islamic principle."
> Al-Hafiz Basheer Ahmad Masri

Why did the rabbit cross the road?

To prove to the raccoon that it could be done.

Since animals cannot speak for themselves, it is all that more important for us to learn to be interpreters and perceive their needs. Being able to perceive the need of another living creature is partly what love is about. It would be fair to say that not all persons, whether they are young or old, truly know what love looks like. Love is having the desire and ability to be there for others. Einstein felt that obligation. He once said that only a life lived for others is a life worthwhile. How many of us can truthfully say that we live our lives for others as well as for ourselves? Could it be that most of us harbor a very selfish (*me* first) attitude?

Of course, when it comes to animals, there are those persons who don't even believe that animals can experience the miseries of excessive heat or bitter cold. They don't believe an animal is capable of knowing that it might be hungry or thirsty. Some persons don't even believe that animals experience fear or suffer from pain. If not, then why will some of them travel many miles in search of water if necessary? Why do animals make every effort to avoid injury or death? If they do not have knowledge, how is it that they find ingenious ways of providing for their own shelter?

"The question is not whether animals can reason or talk, but if they suffer."
Jeremy Bentham 1748-1832

Your Duty

Do you know what a philosopher is, Amanda? Among other definitions, a philosopher is a person who studies human behavior and uses reason, not faith, to search for truth. A philosopher makes knowledge out of reality. There was once a famous philosopher by the name of Emanuel Kant. Although he was born nearly 200 years ago, he is remembered to this day as a great and original thinker, and his teachings changed the lives of millions of people. Kant had two major interests— the heavens above and mankind below. If ever you wondered why you are here... you might find the answer to that question in the words of Kant: "To do your duty." Your "duty" would be to be honorable, charitable, and just. In one word— altruistic. Be there not only for yourself, but for others as well. You are here to do your duty.

And Amanda, have you ever wondered... would this world have been different without you? Then wonder this also: Will this world be different because of you? Will that difference be for better or worse?

"The burden is equal to the horse's strength."
Talmud

Q

What does love look like?

A

It has hands to help others.

Optimists & Pessimists

There's the old joke that says an optimist is that person who wakes-up in the morning and says, "Good morning, God," and that the pessimist upon awakening, says: "Good God, morning!"

A high school band director had once presented a concert that was intended to give his young musicians the opportunity to perform before a live audience prior to going to the state contest. After the concert, he was obviously down in the dumps and someone tried to cheer him up by assuring him that surely the contest performance would be better. He responded by confirming that surely it couldn't be worse. Was he an optimist or a pessimist?

Pessimists act like they think mankind was placed in this world to suffer. Optimists believe that because we're here, perhaps we can bring an end to suffering. Pessimists are grumpy people. They are often times cynical and irritable. Optimists are those persons who are unwavering in their search for the sunny side of life, and they become committed to finding it— for themselves and others. Which of the two personages

39

Ben Garwood

would you rather be?

"To fill the hour and leave no crevices— that is happiness."
Ralph Waldo Emerson

Do You Like To Read?

When you read, you learn. When you learn, you think. When you think, you change. When you change, you mature. This book is about all four of those things... reading, learning, changing, and maturing. There is no magic age as to when the latter takes place. Some adults— whatever their age— show very few signs of ever having matured.

What if none of those things mentioned above never took place? Think about that, Amanda. Think what people would be like if they didn't read, didn't learn, didn't think, didn't change, and didn't mature. Can you imagine? Malcom X who was a well known American political activist once said that without education— no one is going anywhere in this world.

Okay, Amanda, "The time has come," the Walrus said, "to talk of many things. Of shoes and ships and sealing wax, of cabbages and kings— and why the sea is boiling hot and whether pigs have wings." That's from *Through the Looking Glass* by Lewis Caroll. Victor Hugo said the biggest difference in people is found between those who live in light and those who live in darkness. Hopefully, this little book will shine light into your life, Amanda, so read on!

Thomas Jefferson who was a great American president and the author of the Declaration of Independence loved to read. Aside from his love of music and the playing of his violin, he said he couldn't live without his books. Jefferson was so optimistic that he believed all of us were created equal.

41

Alexander Pope who was the greatest English poet of his time, said he loved his books better than his friends. Pope was an optimist determined to change the world for the better. It was Pope who said, "A little knowledge can be a dangerous thing." In other words he was suggesting that it is important to keep searching for the truth.

Ralph Waldo Emerson, said a book is the eye that *sees it all*. Emerson was also an optimist who stressed the importance of self reliance (the map in your head) and who said that nothing could be more sacred than the integrity of our own minds. Integrity has to do not only with the search for truth, but the preservation of truth.

Sometimes young people ask the best questions of all. Recently a girl in middle school asked her teacher, "What can you learn by reading a book about animals?" Well, she will be surprised when she reads this book and finds her question answered many times. You might also be surprised, Amanda, at some of the things you will discover in this book that you didn't already know.

One day, many years ago, I came home from school and my father asked me, "What did you learn today?"

I mumbled, "I didn't learn anything!"

My father looked at me with eyes that could have melted ice and said, "You sat through eight classes and listened to eight teachers talk for fifty minutes each and didn't learn *anything*? You must be pretty stupid. You know Abraham Lincoln said he had little use for anyone that didn't know more today than they knew yesterday.

Now my father had never insulted me like that before and I was dumfounded. If I hadn't learned anything prior to that brief conversation, I learned something then... that I should think before speaking. Of course I had learned things that day. I guess I was so blinded with *attitude* that I just wasn't aware of it. Attitude is one of the demons of self-destruction, you know. Other demons are apathy, indifference, lethargy, conceit, gluttony, and many more. One of the most important things that any of us will ever learn— is how to first identify and then cast out those demons of self-destruction.

The next afternoon when I walked into my father's store, he offered me the same greeting. "What did you learn today?"

I couldn't wait to tell him all the things that I had learned. What a difference a day can make, huh?

Amanda, I know you like to look at books that have pictures of animals, but have you ever had an animal that has been an important part of your life? There are millions of persons, young and old, that consider animals to be a very most important part of their lives.

We'll be talking a lot about different Saints that lived during the past two thousand years. One of them was St. Bernard of Clairvaux who said, "He who loves me will love my dog also." Julian Cutler said he never had a friend more true that his dog. Ebenezer Elliot who was a British Poet said, "If it were not for my cat and dog, I think I could not live." Will Rogers said if dogs couldn't go to heaven— he wanted to go where the dogs go. Abraham Lincoln said, "I care not for a man's religion whose dog and cat are not the better for it."

> "Nothing endures but personal qualities."
> **Walt Whitman**

A Voice From The Past

My old friend Samuel Martin spent hours every day reading books. Sam was a self-educated philosopher who believed that without animals, life would have been a mistake. Whenever he heard anyone express doubt as to whether animals would go to heaven— he would quietly encourage them to be more concerned about the possibility that perhaps it was them who wouldn't be going to heaven while assuring them that their animals would. Many times he would say to someone... "What if your animals go to heaven and you don't?"

In his whole life, Sam never belonged to a church, yet he always discussed religious philosophy... even to those who weren't interested, and Sam believed very much in psychic phenomenon. Once, during a county fair, while volunteering to work in a farm bureau information booth, he took it upon himself to poll of all those who attended the fair. Out of four thousand persons questioned, he said four out of five believed they would go heaven while hardly anyone thought they would go to hell. Among the pet lovers it was six in one hand and a half dozen in the other as to who thought animals would go to heaven.

Sam might best be described as an undiscovered Samuel Clemens. When he wasn't talking, he wrote, even though he never so much as made an effort to publish his beliefs. In all fairness, I must admit he talked incessantly to the point of causing some persons to go out of their way to avoid him. Sam was what many persons would call obsessed. He believed in an afterlife that everyone would eventually reach, and had no doubts as to whether animals were included... but let's start at the beginning.

When Sam was but a young boy, he had a near death experience. When I met him seventy years later that experience was still as real to him as the day it happened:

> "In the midst of life, we are all in death."
> **The Book of Common Prayer**

"You don't ever forget something like that. I can remember starting to fall from the horse, but had no idea as to how I woke up miles away in an old house that had been made into a hospital. When I first opened my eyes, folks were standing around this room I'd never been in before. Some were talking and some were crying. Then someone said, 'Oh Lord, I think he's alive.'

"You can't imagine how astonished I was when I realized they were talking about me. I wasn't surprised that I was alive, rather flabbergasted that I wasn't still what most folks call dead. Just moments before that you see, I had encountered what I can only describe as a voice of light. There were others nearby that appeared to be waiting for me and there were some dogs with them. I didn't know any of them but they all seemed to know me. Wherever I was, it was beautiful and I didn't want to leave, but then here I was again.

"It's hard to explain such an experience, but it was like I had been born for that moment. I had come from darkness into light. I was watching myself be born just like I'd watched the farm animals giving birth so many times when out popped a confused looking little critter to greet the new world. I was confused, but I wasn't scared. I never felt such a peace before.

"Now my papa really wasn't a religious man, but when I told him of my experience, he looked at me in a very weird, yet wonderful way. It was as if he wanted to believe me but couldn't bring himself to do so. Finally he said, 'You'll be alright Sammy. You had a terrible blow to your head but you'll be okay. You just rest and I'll do your chores until you're feeling like yourself again.'"

"I wanted to tell him more. I wanted to tell Papa that I wasn't myself anymore and that never again would I be, but Papa wasn't one to talk to his children unless he was giving instructions. I wanted to tell him that somehow I now knew that when someone dies they are immediately rejoined with family and friends. I wanted to tell him there's no such thing as death. Many times in the years that followed, I would hear Papa tell people that when you're dead you're dead. How I wanted to tell him that we do keep on existing after this life, but I never did.

"What later became the strangest part of that experience was that from the very day of the accident, I seemed to somehow be connected to a thought wave with the animals and what I believed to be the voices of persons I had never known. It was like I could actually hear some of the animals thinking. Animals have a language system within their thought processing capabilities, but it's not about words, rather what they're feeling. Some animals can communicate with one another without uttering a single sound.

My granny died when I was fifteen and after that she talked to me from the beyond. She told me she was now where I had been. That was very interesting since I had never shared that experience with anyone but my father, and yet she knew I had been there. It was then when I began to take a deep and serious interest in spirituality. I even started going to church on my own but soon realized that the preacher had no first hand knowledge as to what he was talking about. He would cite one scripture after another, but he had no idea as to God's compassion and overwhelming understanding for those of us who were temporarily abiding in a body of flesh. I don't know how I knew some things that I knew, but there was a light in me that just kept showing me the way.

"That *light* gave me an awareness of a power that I might otherwise never have known I had. I'd been born in 1870 and only attended about six years of school. I learned to read and write and do arithmetic. I was well enough educated for those times, but although such wisdom is important, I learned that there is a greater kind of wisdom already within us. I somehow knew that by bringing our inner power and wisdom together, we begin to understand who we are and what we're really about. You've heard all these people who say they're searching for themselves? Well they are, but it's difficult to look at one's self and see what's really there. They have no idea as to where they should be looking and it's not in the mirror. One day a great many of them will give up their search without ever having found themselves. What they should have searched for was their inner power and then while combining it with wisdom, spent the rest of their lives using it for doing good. That is the kind of good Jesus was referring to when he said it is more blessed to give that to receive. He wasn't talking about birthday presents, you know."

As a young man, I could not fully understand what Sam was saying to me, but later I read some writings of Meister Eckhart, a religious philosopher born in 1220 A.D. He said that spirituality is not to be learned by flight from the world, by running away from things, or by turning solitary and going apart from the world. Rather, we must learn to penetrate things and find God there.

Has anyone reading this book, learned, anything not already known? Might this book assist in making the penetration Eckhart was talking about—a reality? Was it surprising to hear that Sam found himself in a place unknown and what happened to him after that? Was it of interest to learn that St. Francis talked to the animals? There are actually many people who claim to have the ability to talk with animals. Sure enough. Might that be possible? Remember? The Bible says that Balaam's beast of burden talked to him.

Ben Garwood

"It never ceased to amaze me that the more learned,
the more I realized how little I knew."
Samuel Martin

Language Without Words

During the 20th century, anthropologists discovered and subsequently studied two primitive tribes of uncultured, largely uncivilized, human beings. One was a tribe of pygmy elephant hunters in Africa. The other was a tribe of aborigines in the Amazon jungles of South America. Neither group demonstrated any aggression, but neither yet had a formally developed language system. The aborigines seemed to communicate with a series of tiny, yet articulate sounds. The pygmies substituted the spoken voice for a musical *yodeling* sound. What seemed most remarkable was that this form of communication, although not psychic, seemed almost to be a voice of the spirit. Minus a developed language system, it was as if another sense that might later become replaced with intellectual expansion was serving a function that made it possible for one person to communicate with another.

As we so-called "civilize," and thus intellectually enlighten ourselves in one direction, might it be that we muddy our own waters in another? Do we unknowingly, by our thoughts and behaviors, pollute our own streams? Do we inflict *static interference* upon an innocence that was once the real us?

Scripture would have us believe that Adam and Eve came into creation with a developed language system. After all, they "talked" to God and Eve "talked" to Satan. Anthropologists throw their hands up in despair on that one... knowing that the

51

development of any language is a long and arduous process. But, assuming there was an Adam and an Eve, what if they communicated through a medium other than the spoken word? Do we jostle our true spirit and thus our *power* beyond our reach?

As an animal spiritualist, a state licensed animal rehabilitationist, and an author of animal books, I often come across persons who claim they can speak to animals. They call themselves animal psychics. Allow me to share with you— a very interesting story about a lady who once entered my life:

Her Name Was Jane

Is there really an occult dimension that resides within the human content? Is there an intellectual spook house of clairvoyant, telepathic and sometimes seemingly psychedelic phenomena— a mental order not common to most of us? Is it possible that there are those among us who can unveil a gift wherein powers to expose the unseen and unmask the unknown can intercede on our behalf? Can that force then carry us beyond what we scientifically consider to be the borders of the natural state of our being? If so, what would we call them? Be they fortune-tellers— prophets— mediums— spiritualists— telepathists or soothsayers? Some call themselves psychics, but are they for real? That range of opinions begins with absolutely, and then goes all the way down the thermometer to no way— depending on whom you might be talking to.

Mary does many book signings at various pet expos, and one year I escorted her to the Navy Pier Pet Expo in Chicago. Sometimes I share in the events by autographing my books, but oftentimes I pass the hours visiting the many interesting booths, watching the various animal shows and exchanging conversation with other persons who are likewise professed animal lovers. Among the exhibitors are animal rescue services and those animal angels who represent them— who bring orphaned animals to the events hoping to find compassionate placement for the abandoned ones.

"Are you aware of what that dog is saying to you?" It was a voice that seemingly came from nowhere. I turned my head to see a woman approximately 45 years of age standing beside me and looking at the caged animal before us. "He is speaking to you, you know. He has read your heart and is aware of your sympathy and concern for his plight. He is asking if you would please take him and care for him, and that he in return would serve you with all his might."

What? Who was this self-imposed personage? With a soft and warming smile, she continued. "My name is Jane. There are those who have been certain that I'm the real life, "Plain Jane." She laughed. I was soon to learn there was nothing plain about this woman, and what Shakespeare once wrote about *more things in heaven and earth than ever dreamt of in our human philosophies* was about to take on new meaning. Already, I sensed a power in this individual unlike that of us ordinary mortals. Had I just met a woman who could see beyond the dim unknown— one who could penetrate the darkness that shrouded my own comprehensive abilities?

Some things not to be imagined possible by one person, often becomes the birth of another. Whatever suspicions of fakery I might have once harbored about true psychic ability were certainly reduced to doubts during the next hour that I shared conversation with Jane. She methodically explained how some people are capable of communicating with since-deceased people, but others with animals— not only in the present tense of existence, but even after their death.

I asked her if she believed the psychics who attended the Pet expos were genuine. She told me she could offer no more than an assumption in any effort to answer that question, and that such a determination could only be made on a one by one basis. But she did assure me of her belief that animals and people do have a natural ability to communicate between one another.

Jane continued. "You notice that I did not describe that ability as being unnatural, rather a natural ability, for everyone has it. Animals, you see, believe they have a given purpose here on earth. For some of them, that purpose includes being of psychological and physical assistance to those who directly share love with them. During their entire lifetimes, they attempt to communicate that message and are emotionally debilitated with remorse when their efforts are not successful.

"Some domestic animals express to those who communicate with them, their regret that they have not served well— that their best efforts were unsatisfactory. Yet they acknowledge a realization of being in a learning experience that is comparable to what humans experience in life and thereafter. But draw no early conclusions. Animals do understand death, even though they do not perceive it in the same sense of trepidation as do some humans. The ability of animals to reunite with their human loved one in the dimension after physical death is well within reach, but there are animals, especially those among the wild, that choose to spend their eternity with previous animal friends.

"The important thing to realize [Jane looked softly into my eyes and then spoke again] is that God has a purpose for every single animal that enters our lives. Each animal becomes a very important part of our eternal spirituality and embarks upon a specific purpose in the fulfillment of our own destinies. In a very direct sense, we are one another's mentors. Each of us enriches the spiritual domain of what is to follow.

"Animal emotions are very much like our own. An animal that has been abused either in this or a previous existence is going to undergo a difficult adjustment period in its present environment however defined. This is readily evidenced in the acceptance or rejection behavior patterns of that specific animal. While everyone has the ability to communicate with animals, just like some persons prohibit others from loving them, many never allow that prospect to be fulfilled. Some pet lovers might perceive a facial expression now and then, or a repositioning of the ears or tail, but fail to realize that animals communicate not only with mind, but with entire body language. Very often the animal will dominate the communication if given the opportunity. Sometimes it's more important to observe the hind portion or the legs of an animal rather than the face or forward body for physical indicators that might offer evidence of its willingness to communicate.

"The successful art of such communication is a learning process that takes time and patience. Oftentimes, the animal's brainwave pattern is confused with human demands and questions. When this happens, all possible communication is hindered by a static-like interference."

With a most serious look on her face, Jane said in a darkened tone of voice, "Although there are some animal psychics who profoundly disagree with me, I believe the person who tries to communicate with an animal by listening for mere human words that might come to mind, will be sorely disappointed. Such a communication is more one of emotional telepathy and not dependant on human words. It could be compared to the many non-verbal ways of expressing love, apprehension, fear, hate, hope, or suspicion. If one wishes to think of this science of communication as a language system, then it must be accepted that this is a wholly different approach to the language arts.

"Whereas it is true that we can speak certain words to our animals and they respond— not only to the actual word but even the tone of the voice, this is quite different than the approach through which they can speak to us. In a manner of speaking, it is important that we try to pre-conceive the need or the message. This is not to say we should imagine what the animal might be saying or we will simply be hearing our own thoughts. It is the mental perceptions— the unspoken visualizations that we must learn to perceive. And if there should be those who think animals can provide yet-to-be discovered mysteries of the universal diagram, forget it. Most credible psychics with whom I associate say not even deceased humans have such knowledge, that many on the other side know little more than they knew on this side."

Then Jane abruptly disconnected from the subject at hand and out of politeness said, "My goodness I must be boring you. Please accept my apologies. Sometimes I just don't know when it's time to seal my lips." I assured her that nothing I had heard in a long time held such interest, and asked if she would care to sit in the bleachers and tell me more. She consented.

I asked Jane if she was a psychic, whereupon she tactfully evaded any opportunity to provide me with a direct answer beyond her reassurance that she could communicate with (some) animals.

Jane spoke again: "Would it surprise you to know, that some people can actually find God through the animals even when no other revelations are forthcoming?" Jane paused, but I had no ready response to her question.

"Even though we are but strangers, I will share a portion of my life's earlier experiences with you. Since at least age five, perhaps earlier than that, I was abused in more ways by my father than I care to elaborate on. I share that only because I believe often times it is through that desperate search for love and understanding that the psychic phenomenon within us is released.

"I cannot ever remember having had a mother, and to this day I do not know, nor care to know, the story of my life prior to my existing memories. There had never been mention of God or anything spiritual during my pre-teen years. I did attend school until the middle of my sophomore year, although I had no real friends and was a very poor student. I was never allowed to bring anyone home with me or have any socialization beyond the school day. Since I was withdrawn to being reclusive, scrawny, and quite poorly dressed, I was anything but a prototype that would be readily accepted by one's own peer group. Other than by definition of being my father's object and servant, you might say I didn't even exist. My early life story was no more than a living epitaph of perverse cruelty."

At this moment, Jane's entire physical and emotional countenance changed. She was obviously flashing back into a meaningful era of times past.

"My first spiritual realization came from my father's hunting dog, a creature that like myself was regularly abused— whipped, slapped, kicked, and neglected. It was through the loving eyes of that poor animal when hope first entered my heart and I sensed there might be a greater power.

"I was ten years old— had just endured another of my father's sick inflictions when I escaped his domain of terror by retreating to my hiding place in the barn. There I encountered our dog, Charlie, who was slowly licking those strap wounds within reach of his healing tongue from his most recent beating. Charlie and I often gave meaning to the adage that misery loves company, and we had been friends since he came to us as a puppy some five years earlier. As I sat sobbing in a remote corner, Charlie rose to his feet and slowly limped to my side as if now impervious of his own dilemma. He began licking the tears from my face much like a mother would attempt to soothe a distraught child by wiping away tears with a damp, warm cloth. I looked into his big, sad brown eyes and it seemed as if he was trying to speak to me. I listened carefully and to my surprise I *saw* him say, "Don't give up." Then he lay down beside me and snuggled tightly against me. For the first time in my life I realized I was not alone— that none of us are ever alone no matter how abandoned we might feel, for there is a power to which we are all connected."

There is an ancient proverb that says what comes from the eyes
of
animals is more meaningful than what comes from the speech of
men.

"From that day on until five years later when my father shot Charlie to death during one of his rages, Charlie and I were soul mates. We had communicated with one another that no matter what— when this was all over— that we'd be together somewhere in another time and another place. Three decades have now come and gone, but I still believe that to be true. Charlie not only gave me hope— he gave me peace. I focused my mind on those times to come when Charlie and I would be together in an eternity of happiness. Only another victim of what I endured could even begin to understand, but for the years to come and even now, I can still *see* Charlie saying, 'Don't give up.'

"I wrapped Charlie in my tattered bed coverings and dragged him to the stream where he often went for a cool drink of water to satisfy his thirst on hot summer days. I buried him there with a doll which I was told my mother once made for me. It was my only meaningful worldly possession— all that I had to give him. Although I had never been to a funeral, I made my best effort to speak some words over his beloved remains and assure him he had taught me the most important lesson in life. That lesson is that whenever love is shared, peace can stabilize the spirit no matter what other demons might abide. How I hoped he could somehow feel my words and know how his love for me had offered the only peace I had ever known. Within that same hour, I gathered my items of clothing and began hitchhiking rides from truckers— some who were kind enough to provide me with food and allow me to catch some sleep in the monstrous cabs of their giant eighteen-wheelers."

It is in the gardens of kindness that the seeds of hope are planted.

"Three days later I found myself several states away from the swampy backwaters of that Mississippi riverside town. Now on the outskirts of Chicago—I was penniless and without direction. It is understandable that you would not understand, but

61

Charlie was my guide and still directing me not to give up. I walked into the restaurant of the truck stop where my last ride had come to an end. I approached the counter and asked the man behind the cash register if he could use a waitress. His name was Mel and although he had a somewhat rough look about him, he had an unusually gentle nature. 'You some kind of a runaway?' He asked. Tears streamed down my face and my lips pressed tightly together as I nodded affirmatively. Then Mel said, 'Tell y' what. You go t' that back room there n' clean up some. Then come out here 'n' let's see if you're as hungry as y' look.' "

"I will sing of the mercies of the Lord forever..."
Psalms 89:1

"For whatever measure of time that next expired, Mel sat at a table with me and did most of the talking. He had been a trucker whose wife was killed by a drunken driver. With the insurance settlement, he bought the truck stop that soon became known as 'Mel's Place.' He had no children, no animals, and lived alone in a small house about a mile away from his 'Open 24 hours a Day' business. He was a religious man, who although not a member, regularly attended services at a Seventh Day Adventist's church. After he told me of what a wonderful woman his wife was and how much he missed her, he asked if I cared to tell him something about myself. Well, I guess I just let it all hang out. As he listened to me, I could see the wetness in his eyes and those eyes reminded so much of Charlie's eyes that day he licked the tears from my face. Then, after I could think of nothing else to say, Mel sat quietly without saying a word. I just knew he was going to tell me to leave."

"The calling of one of God's children is the mending of another."

"Mel just sat there and stared into my eyes for what seemed like forever. Then he sort of bared his crooked teeth like a pit bull preparing to attack. In an almost growling tone of voice, he said," 'Know somethin' kid? Around here, you're what folks call jailbait. Kids like you are often handcuffed t' trouble 'n' them what helps 'em, like as not, gets handcuffed t' th' law. But it don't seem fair t' send y'back to that highway, 'cause sure enough you'll soon be climbin' into th' wrong truck what if I do.'

"Then Mel softened. His massive shoulders even seemed to droop as he told me how for a year he'd lived in the back of the restaurant until he got his own place. He said it wasn't a fancy room, but had a stool and a shower— a bed and a dresser and it was private. He told me he'd expect me to earn my keep even though he'd feed me, pay a fair salary, and emphasized that anytime I got the call of the wild, the front door was always open. Meantime, there was one requirement. I had to go to church with him every Sunday. That became my second spiritual experience."

"If the joy of happiness is a great good, the joy of imparting it to others is greater."

63

Ben Garwood

Sir Francis Bacon 1561-1651

"After about two months had passed, Mel motioned for me to follow him outside. He led me to his pick-up truck where he had something he wanted to show me. It was a beautiful mixed-breed puppy that a friend of his who worked for the dog pound had told him about. He cautioned me that I'd have to be careful not to let him get run over in the parking lot while taking him to the back field for exercise. I named him Puddles because he made several of those before I could successfully potty-train him. Puddles became my next experience in psychic communication with animals. Time and again— and I must tell you I first thought it must be my imagination, Puddles seemed to be talking to me. It was not with words from a vocabulary of the vernacular, rather emotions that translated themselves into words. Once I told Mel that Puddles told me he'd like to have a nice fenced-in run. Mel laughed and said, 'He told you that, huh?' I replied, 'Yeah... sort of.' Puddles got his run and a fancy dog house to go with it. Mel was so kind like that in every way. More months passed and before long, Mel had become the father I'd never known. He allowed me to use his charge account to purchase articles of clothing and eventually gave me the title of head waitress. That was quite an honor since he always kept between 12 and 14 girls on the payroll and they were all older than me."

"Happiness is a city of love found within a state of the heart."

"One evening after my shift had ended, Mel called me over to a table where we had one of our frequent talks. He told me how important it was for me to have an education and said he'd be willing to pay for the classes if I'd attend a nearby night school and get my high school diploma. I reluctantly agreed to do so. From there he encouraged me to enroll in a local business college and made his pick-up truck available to me anytime I needed it. Sometimes he would even walk back and forth from home saying he needed the exercise. In less time that I would have thought possible, I went on to a four year college and earned a degree with a double major in sociology and psychology— all the while still calling that little back room at Mel's place— home.

"Time passed. Then on the way back from church one Sunday, Mel said he had to talk to me about something very serious. He confided in me that he had an incurable colon cancer. I cried so hard he had to console me before he could finish. I told Mel he was the only person in my whole life I had ever loved. How I hoped he realized had it not been for him, I might never have known happiness. Mel passed away six months later. More than five hundred persons attended his funeral and in the writing of his own obituary he named me as his special daughter. Mel's love for me didn't end there. Through the inheritance he left me, I was able to receive my Master's in psychology and my PhD in philosophy."

"It is not the vessel that leaves the shore that proves its worth, but the ship that returns to the port."

"Meantime, I had involved myself in animal therapy. I volunteered to take trained animals to children's hospitals and care shelters for the elderly among other places. It was during those times when I further realized I had somehow facilitated the ability to make non-verbal communication with some selected animals. I could actually hear— not through my ears, but in my mind what the animals were saying to their patients. Of course since most persons are ever so skeptical upon hearing anyone make such a claim, I rarely mention it. That's understandable though, because even I find myself doubting some of the animal psychics who claim they can communicate with an animal over the telephone or from great distances. I'm not saying they can't, but I'm far from being convinced, even though I do believe animals as well as people can be communicated with from what we consider to be beyond life. When the most that some psychics can relay is the message that, 'Your animal loves you very much,' I think their communicative skills are weak if not imagined, but when a psychic who has never known the animal or the pet owner prior to the actual communicative experience says, 'Your dog wants you to know how much he appreciated your emotional sacrifices to save his life after he was struck by the bus,' I'm convinced, and such occurrences are frequent."

"Sometimes it is but the smallest piece of evidence
that proves the entire indictment."
Samuel Martin

It was obvious that Jane did not wish to misrepresent the soundness of psychic phenomenon by overstating or understating her experiences. She continued... cautiously.

"It is, in my opinion, important to again reinforce the understanding that what might be described as the animal vocabulary is very small, and limited more to visualization or mental imaging than words. About five years into my present profession as a psychotherapist, I attended a seminar on animal husbandry with a friend. I was astounded at how much correlation was scientifically evidenced between animals and humans. From there I pursued classes having to do with animal consciousness and animal magnetism. I sought any source of knowledge having to do with how animals think, animal self-awareness or animal language. It was almost as if I was being introduced to an undiscovered religion. I learned how some animals had been taught to recognize sign language and how other animals had been taught to recognize symbols and even make assumptions between objects of importance or danger to their natural environment. Some animals even familiarize with faces to the extent of being able to establish immediate visual recognition making it unnecessary for them to rely solely on their malodorous (scent) identification abilities. They can be keenly aware of someone in close association making a change in clothing.

"As much as the expertise those many subjects had to offer, the close association with animal psychologists, researchers, therapists, veterinarians and those specializing in pet behavior problems provided a yet-to-be-defined wealth of knowledge. Much of what I learned was transferable to the needs and treatment of my own patients. Animals are much like humans as they experience many learned behavioral changes during their lifetimes. Some behaviors might be attributed to genetic factors, but other symptoms are clearly attributed to environmental influences. Time after time, the question of psychic ability arose. Now as I believe I already told you, psychic ability is not something that only a select few possess. As a psychotherapist, I believe the potential of psychic communication to be an inherent ability within each of us. It is through that mirror in our soul wherein we can reflect on our yet to be discovered self. "

Since that enlightening and priceless conversation with *Plain* Jane, it has become more than ever obvious that none of us are plain. Regardless of our creed, color, or station in life, we are all blended with the multitudinous experiences of others. Even the least of us has been blessed with gifts we can share with others. Although we are of singular chemistry and physical identities, we are yet spiritually woven together as one in ways unseen. It has now become my fascination to seek the perceptions of those who either claim to be or are believed to be clairvoyant or have whatever facility necessary to communicate with animals. Minus any comments or opinions, here is additional data having to do with psychics— some of which was offered by psychics.

• Some animals are former humans who have returned in animal bodies to assist us during our earthly experience.
• Psychic communication skills can be taught to anyone and the number of such communicators is rapidly increasing.
• Some persons claiming to be animal telepathists also profess the ability to make medical diagnosis of animal illness.
• There are psychics who assert the ability to communicate with deceased animals.
• Although they might insist on their own credibility, there are psychics who concede others are frauds.
• Simply stated, being psychic is the ability to touch the soul or spirit of another.
• I have yet to discover a psychic who claims to be able to predict the time of death of another being—animal or human.
• Some psychics maintain their ability to communicate from great distances.
• One psychic said she can determine the (self-chosen) name of an animal by asking it.
• Animals have dreams similar to human dreams and every dream has a meaning.
• Some psychic hypnotists claim to have taken humans back to animal origins.
• Psychics are not always accurate. Error is possible.
• Everyone is assigned at least one angel, and some human psychics avow they can enable any person to

talk to his or her angels.

Therefore, let it be clearly stated, that wherein there are those who claim to have animal psychic ability, there are others who have investigated those claims and maintain that through their findings no such faculty exists. There are also those persons who practice spiritual healing for animals (humans too). This healing deals with both physical and emotional illness and the healers claim they can administer their powers from remote locations. There are psychics who have been undisputedly debunked— proven to be frauds.

Caution: Deception is not a tool restricted to quacks alone.

Life Dies, What Then?

What really does become of animals after they die? Well, if we turn to the Bible and read Paul's Epistle to the Romans, it says: Not just mankind, but every creature that cometh from God is awaiting eternal life." Elijah Buckner wrote: "Beyond the shadow of a doubt, animals have living souls the same as men." Enoch, who is mentioned in both the Old and New Testaments said, "As there is a special place for all the souls of man according to their number, so is there also of the beasts."

Even so, millions of people don't think animals will be going to heaven. Okay. Billions of people don't think you or I will be going to heaven either, Amanda. (As if they would know?)

> "I beseech you, in the bowels of Christ,
> think it possible that you may be mistaken.
> **Oliver Cromwell 1599-1658**

When someone is close to an animal that dies, a part of their gladness is gone forever. They will think back to the puppy or a kitten times and recall how they watched it learn and grow. They will remember the fun times the two of them shared as well as the dismal concerns brought about by sickness or injury, and once again recall their concern for that pets well being. And most people— will wonder time and again if they will ever be reunited with that animal again.

It is the living who are left to grieve. It is the living

that must suffer the greatest loss. It is difficult to face the realization that physical life does come to an end. Upon the loss of a pet, emotions range from grief and heartache to anger and sometimes relief. Sorrow can quickly turn to anguish and sometimes professional counseling can be beneficial.

At such a time, it is important to focus on the wonderful life the animal was gifted with because of its association with someone who truly loved it. People say that their animal was everything to them— but do they realize they were also *everything* to the animal?

The greatest insult upon the loss of a pet, to the survivor, is in having to cope with those persons who are incapable of understanding the magnitude of the loss. And perhaps the greatest insult to the departed is in saying, "I'll never have another animal. I couldn't go through this again." Then one should ask oneself what the misfortune of some little animal waiting to be adopted might have been had they not brought it home to share love with.

Coping with the loss can be a heavy burden, and muddling through such difficult times can be reinforced through spiritual assurance. Most persons who choose to read a book like this are either already spiritual or searching for the meaning to be found in spirituality. Here again is where *learning* takes center stage. But learning something, about anything, is not always that easy. How many of us might recall how very difficult it was to understand the complexities of the computer? Ask any accomplished musician how many years it took to become skilled on their particular instrument. When it comes to learning— *how to learn* must be as important a consideration as *what to learn.*

How about we learn something having to do with spirituality— right now? When we speak of something being spiritual, we are saying here is something we cannot see as compared to something we can see. It is true that we can say spirituality also has to do with things divine or holy, and we might even think of things spiritual as being of the mind— like a thought. Most important... let's forget about the threat of hell. At least one half of all persons affiliated with convictions of an afterlife believe that everyone will eventually reach salvation. Far better to grasp to that hope as do those of the Buddhist faith who might alone comprise one third of earth's population.

Which persons are most likely to end up in hell?

The ones who thought they could play with fire and not get burned.

There is deep meaning relating to things spiritual. To be spiritual is to believe in an existence beyond this life. I am one who is known to be an animal spiritualist. That means that I believe there is not only a life beyond this life for people, but animals as well. I also believe there is an existing connection between this life and that next dimension.

People often ask me, "Oh, you're an animal psychic?"

No. I am not a psychic. Psychics are persons who claim to have the power to communicate with those on the other side of consciousness. Although from time to time I do strongly feel the presence of humans and animals departed, I cannot speak with them.

Sometimes people ask, "What is the difference in a spirit and a soul?" Although many persons would try to convince me I am wrong in saying so, the truth is that there is really no single or reliable answer to that question. Some people say the spirit is a part of the living body and the soul is a part of the spiritual body. Words, words, words. Of course we couldn't do without words, but people can argue words to the endtime and still never reach common ground.

> "Words are pegs upon which we hang ideas."
> **Henry Ward Beecher**

The difference between spirit and soul isn't of any major importance or consequence anyway. Those are two words that as far as definitions are concerned could be left in the recycle bin of the science of the unknown. It is important not to become influenced by people who don't know what they don't know but nonetheless try to teach it to others.

> Perhaps the greatest threat to truth
> is not an outright lie,
> rather those false persuasions that lead truth seekers away

from their intended destinations.

So many who search for knowledge either base their search on faith or what the majority of other persons seem to believe. Either might well be compared to the Biblical house built on sand. Always remember that no matter how many people might believe something— that doesn't mean it's true. One example of this can be found between those religions that believe in reincarnation and those that don't. Millions believe each way. Whereas about four out of five Americans accept the presumption that there is likely an existence beyond this one for themselves, approximately fifty percent of Americans don't believe animals will have an eternal life. Well, at least they *doubt* it, they say.

> "I try never to be too sure about anything
> because I'm constantly changing my mind.
> I guess the only thing I'm really sure of
> is that I can't be sure of anything."
> **Samuel Martin**

Is it all right to doubt? Stanislaus I of Poland, 18th c., said that to believe with certainty, we must begin with doubt. The next question is how do we turn doubt to realization? How do we find the facts? How do we determine the truth?

Job 2:7-10 tells us to ask the animals:
"Then ask the beasts and they will teach you... likewise the fowls of the air, for they can also tell you. You can even speak to the fishes of the sea, who will declare unto thee that in God's hands

75

is the soul of every living thing."

But how do we *ask*? Is the Bible hinting to us that there are those who can actually communicate with the animals? Was Balaam's beast of burden the first hint of that possibility? Are those who call themselves animal psychics the evidence that such answers can be found through the beasts?

"I have told you earthly things, and ye believe not. How shall ye believe if I tell you of heavenly things?"
Jesus

Faith verses facts. Faith is not fact, yet such a statement is not intended to suggest that one should not consider the faith, beliefs or imaginings, of others. After all, some of the greatest discoveries of mankind began with the fact-finding of a single *renegade* person. It is also important to realize that in many great discoveries, it was the fools that scoffed those persons ultimately proven to be correct. In some instances the ridicule lasted for centuries before the truth emerged. Remember what Sam martin said about "evidence?"

"Sometimes it is but the smallest piece of evidence that proves the entire indictment."
Samuel Martin

Those who search for truth obviously must be numbered among those with faith— because without having faith in what they believe to be fact, their search for truth would never have had a beginning.

Yet— there is a sharp division among those who anchor their faith to mythology and hocus-pocus, incantations and magic powders— compared to those with microscopes and test tubes. Some call it the warfare between Christendom and science. Some believe anyone who is determined to venture beyond simple faith is an enemy of religion. How ridiculous.

"Are they not forewarned by the prophecy of Esajas? 'By hearing ye shall hear, and not understand; and seeing ye shall see, but not perceive.' It is only through the *spirit* in which understanding is to be found."

Yet it seems to the casual and non-biased observer, that when science and religion butt heads— science always seems to be the victor. But surprisingly to many— those scientists are for the most part— not atheists. In days of old and days present, many were and are known by their friends to express deep spirituality in their personal convictions.

Scientists are neither doubting nor denying God, rather if anything, they are proving God. They are removing God from superstition and the hocus-pocus image of Merlin the magician, to a being so magnificent that the human mind is incapable of even beginning to understand what the one commonly called "The Almighty" might really be about.

"In the things of God, knoweth no man."
1 Corinthians 2:11

You see, it is only fitting that it should be the scientists who finally prove the existence of the author of the universe— for God is a scientist... a physicist... an ecologist and an anthropologist. The Creator, is the only one who had the knowledge to systemize the formulations. As for the non-scientific minded among us— they can have *faith* that might be defined as assurance or trust— but in no way can such faith replace fact. Every day, scientists are getting closer to those facts that will prove the existence of the Almighty.

"He that would know what shall be— must consider what has been."
Elliot 19th c.

Einstein said he felt sorry for people who didn't believe in God. As for those who do believe in God, Einstein knew that most of those persons based that believe on faith rather than science, and he found no fault with that. Faith is essential. In the absence of facts, we have *only* faith... but that certainly is not license to give up on additional searches for truth.

"The heavens and earth are full of proofs for the believers. Also in your creation, and the creation of all the animals, there is evidence and proof for those who are certain."
Quran

The Light Of Knowledge
Vs.
The Darkness Of Ignorance

Sometimes all we can do is hypothesize. Now just so we, as author and reader, both know the territory— where we're coming from and where we're headed— let's begin by defining a hypothesis. A *hypothesis* is a proposition used as a basis for reasoning without any credible assumption of truth. Okay? A *hypothesis* is therefore nothing more than a supposition— a possibility that can provide a starting point for further and more detailed investigations. While some might consider any given evidence to be known facts, from a forensic standpoint the best of such presentations might be groundless. Probably what a courtroom would consider to be hearsay if not heresy in days gone by.

A very respected veterinarian by the name of Johns, wrote a book, *All I Need to Know About Living, I Learned From My Dogs*. Some people might laugh when hearing that title, but not people who know and understand animals.

During my high schools years, I had a science and biology teacher by the name of Otto Ohmart. He made such an impression on my life that I dedicated my book *In Search of Truth* to him. Here was a man who could take words and make pictures from them. As if it were magic, he could make what seemed to be the dullest textbooks ever written— come alive with excitement. He taught his students to never believe anything just because someone said it was so. In fact, he was among those who professed that even if everyone in the whole world believed something... that didn't mean it was true.

Now just think about that! Not long ago, everyone thought the world was flat. They believed it was the sun instead of the earth that was rising and setting. Truth is— not long ago, most people didn't do much thinking at all. Another truth is that some people still don't. Unless in your days to come you want to belong to their clubs— you'd better learn to become a truth seeker.

Mr. Ohmart taught us that it would be our own personal choice as to whether we wished to spend our lives in the light of knowledge or the darkness of ignorance. He said that even though one might find what was a "correct answer," not to stop there. A real truth seeker would keep looking for other correct answers. He said not to be discouraged when we might come up with wrong answers, because wrong answers could still represent a search in the right direction. He helped us to realize that no destination can be reached without a beginning. Shall we now look for the light of knowledge having to do with the following quote?

"Beyond the shadow of a doubt animals have the same living souls as man."
Immortality of Animals, Elijah D. Buckner

Upfront

Before we can even begin to approach, much less answer, the question having to do with whether animals can go to heaven, it will be necessary to know something about the people and times of the past. In so doing however, it is important to keep in mind that as Pierre Agustine Caron de Beaumarchais, French author and dramatist observed in the 1700's, many persons don't care if they understand things—they just like to argue about them nonetheless.

While there are those people who would rely only upon the Bible to say animals cannot go to heaven—how about we include the Bible in our sources to prove that they can! It will also be shown how their negative conclusion comes from a misinterpretation of scripture.

"All things bright and beautiful, all things great and small,
All things wise and wonderful, The Lord God made them all."
Alexander 1818-1895

The Bible clearly states over and again that animals will be included in God's plans for an afterlife. Though some seem to have difficulty locating those scriptures, there are countless persons of prominence, including many noted church leaders through the ages who centuries ago arrived at that conclusion from reading the Bible. As many others reached the same assumption from secular (non-religious) sites.

> "It's my guess that when it comes to animals,
> God would give them the shirt off his back."
> **Samuel Martin**

But wait! Let's understand one very important premise from the get go. Even though it includes such commentaries and editorials, the Bible was not intended to be a book having to do with the spirituality of animals. In fact, some of the Old Testament writers believed certain animals to be cursed, which of course was ridiculous. You see, as will be mentioned over and again so that you don't lose sight of that reality— those were very superstitious times. Although some persons have a difficult time coming to grips with the realities associated with such danger-- such superstitions often tended to lead people away from spirituality rather than closer to it. There couldn't be a better recipe for atheism than the stubborn superstitions that still in existence from times close to the days when the dinosaurs walked the earth.

What do some of the age old superstitions have to do with the brain?

Those who believe some of them might be suffering from dementia.

The famous German author, Goethe (1748-1832] once said that nothing could be worse than active ignorance. Just take a look at the world today and see how much active ignorance is alive and thriving... and then imagine what it was like thousands of years ago. And besides— if you had been one of the early Bible writers, would you have been more concerned with the destination of animals beyond this existence— than in developing a working ethical structure among persons who were dying from moral disease and physical starvation? Not likely so.

Nonetheless, animals were popular topics in those ancient times among the general populace. And, although the church shied away from taking an official stand having to with animal spirituality, some of the leaders could see no logical reason why God had created creatures such as flies, mice, serpents, worms, bees, wasps, and others.

"Why couldn't Noah have surmised...
how very wise to have swatted those flies?"
From a marquee undoubtedly edited from a **Helen Castle** quote.

I Am What I Think You Think I Am

Sadly enough, it wasn't just the animals that were looked down on. In times gone by, women were likewise thought poorly of. To state it mildly, it was a man's world. Jesus would have been so disappointed if he had seen how women were treated after his ascension. It was one horror story after another. A sickness of mind!

"Man is not born wicked, he becomes so as he becomes sick."
Voltaire 1694-1778

So animals and women alike fell victim to what might only be described as a sickness of mind. Some people actually thought women and animals to be much the same. It was no laughing matter. The treatment of women was horrifying and what seemed to be a contagious, incurable disease among men. Was it a condition of self-commissioned status or simply a lust for power? One guess would be as good as another.

Had women been given equal rights and allowed to use their minds, likely a cure for the common cold to every disease we are now confronted with would be something only read about in history books. Inventions of the past century would have greeted planet earth centuries earlier.

But it wasn't just the early Biblical era. Even Confucius in the 6th century B.C. had nothing complimentary to say about the women of his times. This phenomenon was more than disrespect. It was male masochist hate and it continued all the way through the Dark and Middle Ages— straight to America. (*Men* were created equal. Remember? And the constitution writers clearly meant *just* men.) Respected leaders of the early church refused to consider that women could have souls or even be human beings, and they orchestrated the burning, drowning and torture to-the-death of as many as a million European women while accusing them of witchcraft. Should we ask those persons who— animals or human—might be entitled to heaven's roll call?

**Why did her dog disappear after the witch used spot remover
to clean some blood from his feet?**

A

His name was spot.

There were many *other than mainstream* beliefs. One is still popular today— even in the Catholic church. It has to do with demon possession and exorcism. Now just how might one get rid of the demons? Why they exorcise them of course. Not infrequently it works, too... but often times by getting rid of the possessed one as well as the invader.

Although demons and their ability to possess the human psyche existed prior to the early church, it certainly found the welcome sign hanging outside every inn. Even many of the early protestant leaders endorsed the certainty of demon possession.

"Could they not see and count all my steps?"
Job 31:4

Animals, Inc.

Guess what? Surprisingly enough, animals were a big part of many particular European societies. There were no vets, but emergency health care clinics and group medical insurance plans weren't available for people either.

Pets were especially sought after by the middle or upper-middle class, and eventually came to be associated with status. Both cats and dogs were popular, but dogs more than cats. Increasingly, some exotic critters as well as horses or other unique and unusual beasts of burden were seen at homesteads in greater numbers. Cats and dogs were purposeful beyond being pets since vermin— rodents such as mice and rats and snakes were nearly impossible to control without the assistance of those two animals. Dogs kept foxes away from the chicken houses and prohibited skunks from living under the sheds. Dogs were also trained for many other needs including hunting.

Why did the snake cross the road?

The chicken had yet to be discovered and Eve was back at the apple tree.

Many families also cherished their pets as friends, surprising as that might seem. There is evidence that the emotional as well as the practical relationship between human and animal was quite favorable. Some Christians who had pets were asking the monks and priests if their pets could go to heaven with them although they found the resulting opinions to be divided. It was also not uncommon for deceased animals to be buried alongside their owners.

Many pets and some beasts of burden were well fed and properly cared for. There were some who held more regard for their animals than for their closest family members or friends. For some persons, an animal was their only outward expression of love. Having to do with concern for animals, a considerable number of church advisers professed proper treatment of animals to be nothing less than a God-assigned duty, but in this respect it seems the pagans might have had the edge on Christians. There were two authors of pagan antiquity, Phthagoras and Empedocles who especially stood firm for animal rights.

Never underestimate the pagans or try to place them in the same category of disrespect that was afforded women or Barbarians who were believed to be the two foremost examples of uncivilized ignorance. Many pagans were religious and worshipped their gods with as much enthusiasm as the Christians worshipped their God— often in a very similar manner. Marriages between pagan and Christians were quite common.

Going back to the most ancient cradles of civilization, we find animals being worshipped by nearly all religions. Many animals such as bulls were considered to be gods, while to the converse, the snake was often the symbol of evil or sex. As those primitive times *progressed* (a poor choice of words) just about every animal imaginable from grasshoppers to falcons and alligators might have been considered holy. Hindus, among many others, believed animals had souls. Snakes, and other reptiles, including rodents, were entitled to temples in some cultures. While people huddled in caves and thatch huts, cows were often held in esteem, second only to God. Some ethnicities envisioned their gods to be part animal and part human. Too bad we can't ask them if both or only one part can go to heaven. Talk about going against the grain... cats became holy in Egypt at a time when rats were ravishing the granaries and the sacred cats destroyed the evil rats.

It wasn't just the Egyptians who loved the cats. In spite of historical sources which testify to the cruelty of some, such as the Spartans sacrificing horses to the god Helios, there is much documentation of love for animals. The Greeks, Romans, and Cretans as well as indo-Europeans held their animals in high esteem. One Roman Emperor loved his horses and dogs so much that he erected tombs and monuments for them upon their death. Those who have read Virgil, the lovable Roman poet who was raised with farm animals, are aware of how he wrote of his fondness for the many creatures. History books are filled with the love of animals by scores of prominent persons from the Middle Ages. From a religious standpoint, those who followed the Talmud were required to abide by strict laws concerning animals— especially if they were used for food, but the love for animals extended far beyond religious guidelines.

And what might have been the relationship between animals and people during the time of Christ? Will you be surprised to learn that people in those times actually shared their living quarters with their animals? Not only dogs, but even sheep were often found as family pets... but what about a "herd" of animals? Sure enough, large numbers of animals were kept inside the house. Sometimes both those of two legs and four legs shared the same space, but usually, the dwelling was constructed so that the animals were at one end and the people at the other. Sometimes the animals were on the ground floor and family living space was on a floor above ground level. Of course when large numbers of animals were boarded within the dwelling, such an arrangement had nothing to do with affection for the animals— rather protection. Animals provided milk and meat. Animals provided clothing, transportation and labor. They could also be raised— traded and sold.

What measure of luxury do your animals enjoy? Each generation seem to have softened regarding compassion for animals. One of my grandfathers who was blind, would never allow an animal in the house. His son, my father let our dogs and cats come in the house but denied them access to furniture and beds.

In our house, one often times has to negotiate with the animals as for a comfortable place on the couch or the bed.

As the ages progressed, artists and sculptors came to realize the affection between humans and animals, and began choosing animals for their primary subjects. Cathedrals were embellished with animal figures carved in stone and animal jewelry became a fashion larger than life. In a manner of speaking, the study and attention given to animals helped transform myth to science as studies of similarities between animal and human anatomy were now being taken seriously.

By the end of the Middle Ages, prominent figures were known to have orchestrated elaborate funerals for their dogs and cats— a practice similar to that of the Egyptians who actually embalmed many of their animals. That, by my observations, likely became the progenitor of pet cemeteries.

During some animal funerals of the Middle Ages, mourners might not only have included members of the Royal Court but surviving animal friends of the deceased pets as well. In some countries, exotic animals were frequently exchanged as gifts, but of course so were women. One well-known animal lover was Tycho Brake (Danish 16th c.) Tycho was one of the greatest mathematician of all times, and although his family hoped for him to become a legal diplomat, he chose astronomy. Yet he was equally known for his love of animals. His was an obsession that ranged from dogs to his pet elk and other unusual beasts that earned his respect and received his attention and compassion. There were ever so many famous and notable persons who were animal lovers. Understandably so, history focuses more on their intellectual contributions rather than their intimacies to the animals.

"Not just mankind, but every creature
that cometh from God is awaiting eternal life."
Paul's Epistle to the Romans.

I'm Sure, I Think

Much of the inconsistency having to do with the perspectives of some persons mentioned in this book can be attributed to changing philosophy or that intellectual ripening that comes with age and thus maturity. But— often times it was not the one time changing of opinion that becomes so noticeable, as the recurrent behavior of switching back and forth from one standpoint to another. Such discrepancy often had to do with the inability to break away from earlier certainties and convictions— even in the face of evidence. Old sureness of mind could and did erase reason.

Anyone who studies the life of St. Thomas surely will note that he seems to be a leading person in point who had a difficult time making up his mind. It seems to me that Thomas, especially Thomas, went back and forth regarding his belief about animals having souls. He seemed to be confused with scripture that suggested animals died as a single unit with their body, and yet he could not help but entertain what finally appeared to be his greater belief that animals would receive a revivification— a renewal into a new life form apart from the physical body. Of course there is nothing wrong in contradicting oneself— especially upon having discovered a new truth, and there is no person to be more admired than he or she who will admit error while attempting to make amends with the newfound reality.

"Do I contradict myself? Very well then I contradict myself.
I am large. I contain multitudes."'
Walt Whitman

VOLTAIRE

Allow me to introduce this most unique individual, 1694-1778, by saying here was the man who wished to discover the steps from which to determine how mankind progressed from barbarism to civilization. Even after having studied Voltaire in college a half century ago, there is still a compelling interest to examine this man's writings. Such findings might occasionally substantiate the professor's lectures on Voltaire's spiritual beliefs yet sometimes do not. Once again we're caught-up with interpretations. The different way of saying things from Voltaire's times to ours renders some of his communication so intrinsically complex that it is a bit difficult to understand what he actually does profess. Therefore I will relate what that college professor espoused to her classroom nearly five decades ago having to do with Voltaire regarding his theory about animals and souls in general.

Due to the influence of this very knowledgeable lady-educator, I do believe Voltaire to have been an animal lover by every facet of the imagination. She assured us that Voltaire despised anyone who would harm an animal for any reason whatever, that they did have souls, and that early on he noted animals are capable of demonstrating nearly every emotion that

94

might be expressed by human beings.

How exciting it would be to discuss Voltaire's beliefs having to do with the soul in person and in today's manner of speaking. I would ask: Do you believe the soul something having to do with the physical body or is it beyond flesh, blood, tissue, and bones? Did the soul precede us? Did the soul come into existence upon conception or at the time of birth? Did the soul come later? And what about all those little swimmers in the sperm that never made it to shore or aborted babies? Did they have souls?

> "There is nothing which God cannot effect."
> **Cicero**

Now Voltaire wasn't even his real name, rather a pseudonym the man must have coined for himself. He was of a character that would certainly have made him a political activist in our times, yet apparently he was as outspoken having to do with the rights of animals as for the rights of his fellow mankind. Was he meek? About as much so as a water buffalo. He was a rascal to say the least and because of his forthright, blunt and candid ways, he once spent nearly a year in prison. In spite of his literary genius, he was ready to pick a fight with anyone who dared mistreat an animal or who might profess that animals were but dumb beasts that could not experience pain and suffering.

Voltaire emphatically repelled any notions suggesting animals were ignorant creatures of lesser worth and said those who so believed were but describing their own mentality. Among his society at large, there was widespread agreement that since non-human creatures were of lower intelligence, they did not suffer pain or emotional anguish. Voltaire, however, knew that animals suffered from pain and emotional anguish. He also believed animals could reason— distinguish some rights from wrongs and even be aware of their own wrongdoings.

According to my professor, whose only apparent love in life was her poodle. Voltaire positively believed animals to have souls. In fact, she insisted that aside from his more than fifty plays and other writings, he found it his duty to offer extensive knowledge to the world of his times as to what a soul consisted of. He did allow, however, that it was beyond any man's ability to accurately define a soul. Whereas some believed the soul to be a physical or material substance within the body, Voltaire insisted it was no more of a tangible substance than a thought. He was once asked by a group of his skeptics whether the soul of a genius and the soul of an imbecile were of equal worth. Such persons of course were linking soul to brain. Voltaire believed that anything possessing a soul, animal or human, could not be divided from its consciousness, and according to the professor— Voltaire believed there might be those animal souls that were of more value to their creator than some human souls.

"The Bible tells us how to go to heaven, not how the heavens go."
Galileo

Descartes

Whether or not one might support a particular truth-seeker's belief system, it is necessary to examine all perspectives of view. Descartes, 17th c. attempted to do just that. Descartes, like myself, numbers among those who often combine God, humans, and animals into related subject matter. In his writings, "Meditations of First Philosophy," he elaborates on the existence of a Supreme Being, and delves into the difference between soul and body. He shares his findings having to do with animal thought processing capabilities, though he might not always confirm what others might wish to hear, he does allow that since animals can think, they surely do have eternal souls. Interestingly so, he then examines the difference between instinct and intelligence.

Descartes is best known to some for his infamous, statement: "I think, therefore I am." Samuel Martin once said: "Sometimes I think and do it and sometimes I just do it and then think about it." Could that be the difference in instinct and processed thought?

"How many persons have noticed how readily we embrace others
whose beliefs agree with our own but how we avoid them when they
think differently than we have been taught?"
Samuel Martin

Stories & Storytellers

Since the earliest of recorded history, people have always been drawn to persons with stories to tell. Actually, that's what historians are— *storytellers...* but do the tellers of tales always tell the truth? Sometimes, word of mouth narratives are not supposed to be actual truths, rather situations that enable those listening to the stories to see an event more vividly. Such yarns are often called fables or fairy tales. They are make-believe circumstances of something that *maybe* really was or at least *might* have been. It is also possible, of course, that such accountings could portray more reality and knowledge than if one had witnessed an actual happening.

To **be**lieve or not to **be**lieve. That is the question.
"Doubt is often the first step to truth."

1

**What was it that the bee philosopher never could decide
upon?**

A

To bee or not to bee.

A historian should always tell the truth— the whole
truth and nothing but the truth although that is
oftentimes far from what some historians represent. It
seems that many of them actually want to reshape
history to what they wish it had been or to discredit
someone or something else. There are those
historians who actually seem to be killing history
rather than preserving it. That is why one cannot
always assume what is being stated is what really
happened.

"Doesn't matter what we think we might know about things—
it's only a fool that won't take his hat off in the face of facts."
Samuel Martin

It is important to be able to separate actual events
from traditional legends or folklore. Maybe we aren't
expected to believe that the frog actually turned into a
handsome prince when kissed by the beautiful
princess. Instead, we might philosophize that the
goodness represented by one person (or a group of
persons such as the Seven Dwarfs) helped a less
fortunate being to experience a better existence. *The
Book of Mencius* teaches that: "The greatest man is

99

he who does not lose his child's heart." It is with our child's heart that we read and understand the values that are taught by many of those stories of old. (Mencius was a Chinese Confucius philosopher.)

There are so many *stories* such as Jack and the Beanstalk, The Sleeping Beauty, Cinderella, Little Red Riding Hood, Hansel and Gretel, The Beauty and the Beast, The Pied Piper of Hamelyn. The Goose Who Laid the Golden Egg and countless others. Although these stories might teach values, they would not be found in a bookstore's non-fiction section.

Many such stories are about animals. Sometimes the animals are the heroes and sometimes they are the villains. One of the most respected animal storytellers of all times was a man, previously mentioned, known as Aesop. Aesop was a Greek slave that lived some 600 years before the birth of Christ. Because of the fame Aesop received from telling his stories and because of the principles his stories represented, Aesop was finally freed from slavery.

There are also many Christian stories having to do with animals, although the story of Noah's Ark is probably the best known. Throughout the Bible, one reference after another is made of animals. Among the first sounds that Baby Jesus ever heard came from the lowing of the cattle. When Christ was born, shepherds were nearby watching over their flocks of sheep and this long awaited for Messiah was said to be the Lamb of God. Can you imagine that they would have referred to Jesus as a Lamb?

Was Joan of Arc Noah's wife?

$\mathcal{A}$

No. That was Joan of Ark.

There have always been animal stories galore-- and so many sayings having to do with animals. Take for example, "It's raining cats and dogs." In the old Norse stories, the god of storms was always accompanied by a dog, and the witches in the middle ages that were accused of causing storms rode on their brooms disguised as black cats. Fantasy? Yes. But let's take a venture:

Fantasy vs. Reality

For sure, through all the ages, animals continued to be popular topics in the midst of the spiritual and non-spiritual alike. Some loved animals while others feared and dreaded them. There were those who worshipped them and yet others thought them to be associated with demons. Still another number of persons seemed to pursue anything having to do with animals even if considering them to be despicable and unworthy beasts.

Although the church might have taken no official stand having to do with animals, many church leaders could see no logical reason why mice, frogs, serpents, worms or various insects such as flies, bees, wasps and others had been created. There were no ecologists at that time to explain the balance of nature, so why else would the hurtful animals have been created if not to keep mankind from enjoying life too much? One well known religious man who loved, respected, and defended most animals, believed the fly was sent by the devil to annoy him when studying the Bible, and he believed rats to have been demon-possessed.

> "Truly, when it comes to superstition,
> even wise men follow fools."
> **Francis Bacon**

Most religious and non-religious people believed in dragons, but understandably so. After all, the Bible confirms dragons: Duet. 32:33, Psalms 91:13, 74:13, 148:7, Isaiah 27:1. The Chinese could boast dragon stories going back untold thousands of years and numerous Western culture chillers had plenty tales of their own. Could ancients have confused dinosaurs with dragons? Thought them to be one and the same?

Church leaders and other prominent persons of knowledge also believed that an animal known as a basilisk (see dictionary) that was somewhat related to the dragon but had a tongue of stone could kill other serpents by its very breath. Not only that, but if it drank from a body of water, the remaining water was said to become poisonous to others. By simply crossing through a forested area, the entire area of vegetation might become a desert and thus at least one supposed, yet non-scientific, origin of the deserts. This basilisk was said to have been an animal of about four feet in length, similar in appearance to an alligator or crocodile. According to all eye-witnesses, it was nothing less than a giant lizard that some believed to possess intellect superior to that of humans. For certain it must have contained powers beyond imagination, since it could kill a human with a mere glance from its piercing eyes. Fortunately, as history records, the Pope saw to it that all basilisks were destroyed with prayer, the sign of the cross, and the help of a crucifix. One cannot help but wonder with tongue-in-cheek— had it not been for such miracles, would the world's entire human population have become extinct?

Other animals to be feared were the behemoth and the leviathan, Job 40 and 41, Psalms and Isaiah. There was also a bird called the Phoenix— a mythical creature of flight that lived among other places in the Arabian barren wastelands. It made its nest from frankincense and myrrh and was believed to have had a life span comparable to the pre-Noah (human) times. Yet, prior to its demise, it could dive into the flames and ashes of bodies being cremated and experience restored youth that concurrently provided it with another cycle of life. The contemporary usage of the name, Phoenix, is taken from that bird's amazing ability to recover from certain doom by the power of miracles.

There were other fabled animals such as the gargoyles and all sorts of half man, half beast ogres. Wonderful myths, but so many persons upon listening to those mythological stories turned them into truth serums and injected them into the minds and therefore the belief systems of all who would listen. There were at least two stories having to do with whales, and one such story included in an early Psalter told of a giant whale resting on top of the waters for such an extended period of time that grass grew on its back. Some sailors thinking they had located an island climbed onto the whale and made a campfire. The annoyed whale dived deep into the sea and drowned all the sailors. Fiction and miracles could be much likened to narcotics— a quick fix for bored or troubled minds in otherwise intellectually and academically uninteresting times. How can one help but lay awake at night while wondering if the basilisks and the dragons went to heaven with the other animals?

Perhaps those who are perceptive are also beginning to realize why there wouldn't have been much concern for the spirituality of animals during these eras of animal fables.

What was it that always followed the mythological animals around?

Their "tales."

Numerous stories, legends, and superstitions abounded. It was well known that certain animals could not be pursued by predators, since some having dragon-like tails were smart enough to swish their tail about and conceal all tracks. The cat, never mentioned in scripture, as well as other animals was suspected of being a link between Satan and the witches. There were those who believed that creepy animals such as vampires fed their young with their own blood that had been drawn through hollow fangs from the bodies of other living beings. Dragons also, were known to be the helpmates of Satan in his continuing war against the children of God.

"Why are we so constituted that we believe the most incredible

105

Ben Garwood

things, and once they are engraved in our memory, woe to him
who would endeavor to erase them.'
Goethe 1774

There were animals considered capable of eating
and thus breathing fire, while some were said to be
able to talk with humans. One eerie species of bird
was believed born from the fruit of a tree when the
seeds hatched after coming into contact with water.
Does anyone feel further need to determine if those
who believed such things, had adequate knowledge
to declare whether animals might or might not go to
heaven?

Disco Primo quod credendum est
"Learn first what is to be believed.'
Hugo of St. Victor

Why couldn't the dragon get rid of his migraine headaches?

He ate the vet.

Lincoln believed it possible to fool all of the people some of the time and perhaps he was correct, It seems there are things that even those assumed to be the intellectually elite are superstitious enough to believe. Samuel Martin said the best stories based on myth were to be told by those persons who really believed them. Wouldn't it be fun to hear the original storytellers describe having seen those animals that had foreparts of one species and hind parts of another? This combination of anatomy was often half giant insect and half mammal. Some had dragon's heads with horse bodies and others had two heads. Of course the mermaid was an even greater exaggeration.

Many were the tales about creatures that could swallow men whole and then weep inconsolably for having committed the deed. Many of those who believed in dragons were convinced they were born of fire and resided deep in the earth. Biblical naturalists of the day were undoubtedly swayed by the continuous stories of fighting between large menacing beasts and dragons. The stories of horror from first-person eye-witnesses were told in precise detail while

Ben Garwood

their imaginings were well illustrated in the writings and drawings of others.

No, it wasn't the Age of Science— it was the Age of Stupidity, more courteously known as The Age of Faith, and sometimes the bigger the whopper, the better. No matter who was telling the stories they usually got better each time they were told.

Meantime, the church in this Age of Faith is preparing to enter another crusade that will become a war of wits with the soon to arrive Age of Reason. Many will soon be asking the most ridiculous question of all... why anyone would resort to reason (proof) when they have faith? After all, as some will argue: Way back fourteen ninety two, Columbus sailed the ocean blue. He didn't know where he was going and when he arrived he didn't know where he was. Worse yet, when he returned he didn't know where he'd been... but his faith kept him going. Well, so did his compass, his well-engineered ships, his olde world primitive maps and his studies of many years. Faith plus science can make for a winning team!

2 Corinthians 5:7 says we walk by faith— not by sight. Beautiful words, but remember that Christ had to show the disciples the nail prints in his hands before they would believe.

The Great Spirit

Perhaps you have seen the poster that says *America is the greatest country ever stolen by anyone.* Although that slogan might have been intended to portray a tiny bit of humor, there is also both truth and sadness in those words.

When the White man first initiated behaviors that became the beginning of the end for the culture of the Native American Indians, the Indians watched in disbelief. Herds of animals were being slaughtered for mere recreational delights— shot from passing trains for mere target practice. Forests were being cut down, villages destroyed and their people dehumanized or murdered. Still, to many of them the greatest insult of all was that this same invader was making mockery of their spirituality and their practice of worshipping the Great Spirit.

My genealogy is somewhere between a mixture of various flavors and varieties, but as best can be determined contains a maternal native-American descent of Cherokee, French Mohawk, and Apache. I guess that makes me a mutt? Due to that lineage, there has always been an interest to learn as much as possible about the American Indians. Upon hearing the White man's vision of heaven, an Indian might have replied:

You tell me that your land beyond the sun is a heaven with
golden pathways.
Are your heavenly trails more splendid than those

made by the moose and the antelope?
Does the call of the coyote and the hoof beats of the
deer mule
echo from the bluffs of your heaven?
And does the cry of the gliding bird answer him?
Do the buffalos roam your plains?
Can I still feel the warmth of the sunshine against my
face?
Can I hold the wind in my hands?

Through the psyche of any Indian's imaginings, might we not therefore assume that heaven to him would not be heaven without the animals?

"In my father's house are many mansions."
Jesus Christ

Tell Me The Tales

According to everything within memory's reach having to do with what my Indian Grandfather shared with me, the native-American Indians treated their animals with utmost respect and consideration. Although not a hunter, Grandpa often recited what he called, "The Indian Hunter's Prayer," which went something like this:

> Deer, I am sorry that I must hurt you.
> I am sorry that you will no longer sip from the cool streams
> or race as the wind across the open plains.
> I regret you will no longer share the seasons with your brothers,
> but my people are hungry and I must feed them.

Many tribes of American Indians placed Divine reverence on that previously mentioned Great Spirit. They believed in the certainty of another world to come wherein they would be with that force. In the varying Indian cultures there was much emphasis placed on spirits-- both ancestral and animal spirits alike. Many Indians made pets of dogs, and even of raccoons, opossums, and birds, but all animals played an important role— not only from the Indian's concept of the creation and creator, but to the happenings of their everyday lives. Some believed the earth rested on the back of a giant turtle, while others believed it was carried through the universe by a great bird such as the thunderbird that represented superior strength and stamina.

Many Indians might have traced their origins to a single ancestral animal such as a wolf or a fox, and thus remained a soul brother with that animal for life. But what represented a belief system for one Indian tribe was not necessarily the same for another. Their beliefs, like their languages, were multiple. American Indians might have had as many as 700 different languages represented among their various tribes.

"I do not wonder what the Great Spirit requires of me. I know."
Aiwana

The buffalo, brought to the brink of extinction by the White intruders, were revered by many Indians as their primary substance of life. Indeed, for many tribes-- their very lives depended upon the buffalo that some tribes believed spiritually sacrificed itself for their survival. Each single part of that animal's anatomy was used for every imaginable purpose. Was it any wonder that Indians fashioned altars and held ceremonies in honor and respect for that marvelous animal provided to them by the Great Spirit? From what Grandfather spoke of the Indians, it would have been rare to find one that was not an outdoor enthusiast-- a lover of nature so to speak. Whether or not some might have been considered animists, Indians were indeed naturalists and environmentalists who believed themselves to be one and the same with nature and the animals. Are we not also? Jesus did ask, "Know ye not, ye are gods?"

"It is by the will of the Great Spirit that the skies, the mountains, the waters and all life on earth came to exist."

Aiwana

Some Indians believed that both humans and animals were involved in an ever-recurring reincarnation-like cycle of birth and rebirth. As the Christian Bible suggests, the stranger at the door might be the Lord in disguise. There were some Indians who believed certain animals could have been the Great Spirit in subterfuge.

Following the hunt, it was common practice for some tribes to return the bones and other parts of animals sacrificed by the kill to nature by burial. It was believed that such an entombment would ensure survival of the animal's soul. It was not uncommon for an Indian to wear a part of a deceased animal— perhaps a bone, a tooth or claw, even part of the skull— having to do with a spiritual bonding of the animal.

"Why is it that those of the pale faces wished to change the order
of my people?
We did not so disrespect them."
Aiwana

Many Indians respected not only the animals but the very vegetation and soil as well. It is surprising that since Genesis says our human physical components come from the soil, that the white man's culture does not revere planet earth as did the red man. Many Indians, as do some naturalists today, believed trees and plant life to have been sacred, and that to needlessly destroy any part of nature was to reject the creator's gift. Did the Indians believe that

113

animals would be resurrected and with them in *The Happy Hunting Grounds?* Yes, most did.

Remember that story about *footprints in the sand?*
What if God's *footprints* turned out to be *pawprints?*

Man's Best Friends

Since there is so much Bible talk about animals -- stories galore-- those writers of the gospels must not have thought anything having to do with an animal to be inconsequential. Consider just a few... Jon and The Little Lost Lamb, Noah's Ark, Daniel in the Lion's Den, The Man Swallowed by a Fish, Stories of the Fishermen and so many others. Aside from the Bible, there were other sources referring to animals, such as the one about Gerisimus the Abbot. Gerisimus was the monk who healed the lions paw by the river Jordan. True, the story was very similar to an earlier one told by Androcles in the 1st century, but even if such tales might have been repeats, they were nonetheless filled with moral values.

Although Genesis says that man was to have dominion over the beasts, imagine how the chapters of history would have been changed had it not been for those animals. In some areas of the world, man could not have survived without their contributions. Not only did the animals provide food and protection for mankind, they were the beasts of burden from the earliest annals of recorded history. Imagine their ability to reassign their instincts and non-domestic lifestyles to be of service to mankind. Animals carried the cargo across the dry land, they turned the grinding wheels, and caravans of animals provided transportation for humans across the most rugged terrains in all extremes of weather and climate. Were not the lands of milk and honey considered to be

Ben Garwood

among God's greatest blessings, and did those blessings not come from the milk-producing animals and the bees?

But the blessings from God's gift of animals far exceeded milk and honey. There was cheese and meat which offered dietary substance to even those persons of pre-Biblical times, not to mention clothing, shoes, carrying sacks, shelter from hides and even liquid-containers within which they could safely enclose and transport water.

"We should remember in our dealing with animals
that they are a sacred trust to us from our heavenly Father.
They cannot speak for themselves."
Harriet Beecher Stowe

Each Unto Its Own Kind

Albert Einstein, as well as sociologists and others, observed from time to time that as human beings we are a part of the whole, and yet we often envision ourselves to be something disconnected from the rest. Could not being part of the whole be said of animals that seek association with their own kind? Consider the many birds of a feather that flock together... the schools of fish, the onetime herds of buffalo, wild horses, dog packs, ad infinitum. Yet how quickly some of them accept separation from their own kind and willingly become part of our lives. If extraterrestrial beings of superior intellect came to earth and abducted us as pets, would we so willingly adjust?

To my perceptions, one conclusion made by that great man, a physicist who became the Father of Atomic Energy was that our task must be to free ourselves from what can become a self-imposed prison. We must learn widen our circle of compassion to embrace all living creatures and the whole of nature in its beauty. Many of the Native American Indian tribes certainly ascribed to that philosophy.

"The universe is a single life comprising one substance and one soul."
Marcus Aurelius

117

Birds of a Feather

How important are animals in your life? Do you love animals? Do you have an animal that loves you? At this very time, about 36% of American families own a dog and 32% have a cat. Of course there are countless other kinds of animals that help to make a house, "Home Sweet Home." Many persons are attracted to birds— birds that live outside and birds that live inside.

Do you enjoy the Robins, the Bluebirds, and the Cardinals? Do you enjoy the birdsongs of the feathered flying animals? Do you like to see the wild geese fly? Have you ever fed the ducks or watched a wild turkey in search of food?

Maybe you've heard someone kidding another person by calling them a birdbrain? Well, you know, that could actually be a compliment.

Tweet, chirp, zeet, teet, ch-ch-ch-chirp. The Bible mentions many kinds of birds— all sizes and shapes. One of the most interesting is the kite, from which today's 'kites' take their name. The kite mentioned in the Bible had a wingspread of approximately four feet and a body that was almost two feet long. There were also cuckoos, owls, ravens and hawks— storks, peacocks, turtledoves, quail, and vultures. Elsewhere, scripture tells of birds or birdlike creatures such as bats (mammals) and ostriches.

And as for birdbrains? Some birds, such as parrots, can count and some can imitate human speech. Many species of birds can solve complex puzzles that some humans of supposedly normal intelligence cannot disentangle. Have you ever attempted to build a bird nest? To what do you anchor those very first twigs? Try it— and be sure not to use any utensil other than a single pair of tweezers in imitating the bird's beak. What the birdbrain can do is astonishing.

Q

The Vatican once had a parrot that had been trained to recite the Lord's Prayer whenever anyone pulled on its leg. Fascinated, the Pope could not help but wonder what would happen if he pulled both legs. Do you know what happened?

A

It fell off its perch.

A man we'll talk about later on named St. Francis considered the birds to be his little *sisters,* and he often reminded them to praise God for having been given the freedom to go any place they wished. Yes— Francis of Assisi, who is the Patron Saint of Animals often talked to his birds.

We could rightfully call St. Francis the Birdman of Assisi, but there was another birdman in more modern times known as the Birdman of Alcatraz. Believe me— they had nothing in common other than birds, for Alcatraz was a prison. Actually, the Birdman of Alcatraz earned his title during his thirty years at Leavenworth prison, where he raised hundreds of birds, studied cures for their diseases and wrote two books prior to being transferred to Alcatraz.

Want to know more about what the Bible has to say about birds? Read Num. 11:31, Ps. 104:17, Gen. 8:7-8, Psalm 102:6, John 18:27, II Chron. 9:21, Luke 2:24, Matt. 3:16, Isa. 34:14, Psalm 84:3, Isa. 40:31, Lev. 11:13-19, Matt. 10:29, Isa. 34:15, Luke 13:34, I Kings 17:6, Job 39:13-14.

> "On that I had wings like a dove,
> For then I would fly away and be at rest."
> **Psalms**

Animal Sacrifice

It's a bitter pill to swallow, but there is much evidence showing the sacrifice of animals has not been something limited to the primitives. From the most ancient to modern times, animals have literally existed under the whip and suffered until being worked to death. Even today, in many parts of the world, such animals still function as beasts of burden. Some persons use animals in sports— some of which are unconscionably cruel such as bullfighting, cock fighting and dog fighting. It seems to come with the (mental) territory. Some people of course even like to watch people fight other people. Is such a desire connected to a primitive gene?

Are animals, by some bizarre doctrine of predestination, here to experience birth, suffer both nature's hardships and man's evils just to exit life into nothingness— non-existence? No reward? What kind of creator could do that?

After affording careful thought and study to the love of the Creator, how could anyone be so stingy of heart that they could possibly endorse an all time termination for any creature? Consider the 200 million helpless animal victims, many of which are primates, that perish yearly in painful scientific experiments after suffering day and night for months... sometimes for years.

Animal research can be of value by enabling scientists to find cures for diseases and even bringing us to a greater understanding of things such as the aging process. But should human beings force innocent animal beings to endure indescribable pain and physical deformity— especially for nothing more than developing new cosmetic products? Vanity, vanity. Does not some animal research constitute cruel and inhuman behavior? Proverbs 21:3 reminded those of days gone by that God does not desire animal sacrifice. Perhaps with other than a few exceptions, mankind still stands in need of such a reminder today.

What is additionally perplexing, is that many animals are sacrificed to find cures for the diseases that result from humans having eaten them.

If you'd care to help those innocent animals, contact the ASPCA: www.aspca.org or 424 East 22nd St, NY,NY 10128-6804. Arthur Broome, an Anglican Priest founded the first Society for the Prevention of Cruelty to Animals in England in 1824.

Samuel Martin once said that even though the defenseless animal cannot speak on its own behalf, that the God of life hears its helpless voice nonetheless. He added: "Think not that the time of judgment is not drawing near." That silent voice also comes from the millions of animals that die from thirst, cramped conditions, freezing to death, and suffocation while on the way to the slaughterhouse.

Mary and I once stood in helpless agony as we witnessed a truckload of cattle, some already frozen and others slumped to their knees --half frozen-- while on the way to the slaughterhouse in −25' temperatures that did not include wind chill or the added wind exposure due to the not-fully-enclosed truck. Sure hope those ribs, steaks and hamburgers made someone happy!

And then there are the pet markets that are also participants in the cruel and couldn't care less methods of animal transportation. Beautiful Amazon birds for example, stuffed into tight containers while unable to move even their head, and incarcerated for extended periods of time with no food or water.

Still another five million U.S. animals per year are trapped, drowned, callously and maliciously mangled for their furs— in spite of the fact that the average yearly profit to the trapper is less than $300. To make one single 40-inch fur coat from an animal of a single species requires the fur of 16 coyotes, 18 lynx, five dozen minks, 20 otters, 45 opossums, 42 foxes, 40 raccoons, 50 sables, 8 seals, 50 muskrats, or 15 beavers.

If that is not sacrifice enough, another 150 million U.S. wildlife animals annually fall victim to those brave and fearless hunters who with telescopic scopes and the most advanced of high-powered weaponry burn hot balls of fire into the unsuspecting, innocent and defenseless wildlife— taking their only possession, the precious gift of life itself away from them. Add to that the lost companionship of their animal friends that cared for and shared life with them. And how proud those huntsman are for doing to another what an invisible germ-- or cancer might one day do to them (as was stated in the foreword of this book). As far back as the 16th c. B.C., Pythagoras said that as long as men massacre animals, they sow the seeds of murder and pain, and themselves will never escape torment or reap love and joy. Mohammed condemned animal fights, animal imprisonment, and the wearing of animal skins.

There are of course two sides to every story. One of my friends since childhood is Philip Ferrill who now lives in St. Louis, Missouri. He also owns property in the Ozark regions of Missouri and is an avid hunter. What? This animal lover would actually call a *hunter*— friend? Of course! Doesn't the Bible teach us to hate the sin but not the sinner? Well, let's not even go so far as to call Phil a *sinner* even though that particular aspect of his life is very opposite from that of mine. In fact, it is important that the hunters do have an opportunity to be heard from in this book, and there could be no better representative of their voice than Phil Ferrill. Here is a portion of a recent letter received from Phil.

Dear Ben,

While traveling from Europe, I read "What In Heaven's Name." I have recognized for decades that there are a lot of people who do not hunt and do not approve of those of us who do. I have always tried to understand and respect their point of view and ask in return that they pay me the same courtesy. I especially respect persons such as you and Mary who do not eat meat. In my opinion, it is a hypocrite who criticizes hunters but doesn't mind eating meat as long as someone else does the dirty work of killing the animal.

I understand that it must be very difficult for a non-hunter to understand how someone like myself can love animals and still kill them. Seems like an oxymoron doesn't it? I guess it all boils down to the difference in what we believe God intended for our relationship with animals to be. I believe that God intended for animals to fulfill more than one roll. Animals are beautiful creatures that each have their place in the balance of nature in the food chain as well as in their domestic relationship with man. While nature is fascinating and beautiful, it is also hard, cold and cruel. Any bird or animal can be prey/food for some other bird or animal.

I believe that we are at the top of the food chain due in large part to some unfair advantages. We appear to be more intelligent, most of the time. This intelligence has allowed us to develop tools and weapons that the rest of the animal world doesn't have. However, along with this 'advantage' comes responsibility.

I, and the people I hunt with, hunt within the applicable laws. We only kill what we eat. We make every effort to make clean kills so that the animal doesn't suffer any more than is absolutely necessary. We have a great respect for nature and actively engage in conservation practices.

It gives us comfort knowing that the fees and taxes we pay to participate in the sport of hunting go toward good conservation practices. Under the current system, were it not for the hunting and fishing fees and taxes on related equipment, there would not be adequate funding for necessary conservation efforts.

There is also the fact that animals can reproduce more rapidly than the land can support. Hunters harvest the surplus. Of course it is true that this is due to the fact that man has also eliminated most of the predators that used to take care of that 'surplus.' Still, if we didn't harvest the surplus, Mother Nature would dispose of it in a much less humane manner than does the hunter. The surplus animals that the land could not support, would die from starvation and disease. Meantime, the farmer's crops would be decimated while hungry and bewildered animals would be causing additional motor vehicle accidents that would result in cruel deaths of animals and humans alike.

I hope what I have written sounds rational. You know that I am an animal lover, and in fact would like to contribute a wonderful story about a basset hound named Flash to Mary for consideration in one

Ben Garwood

of her upcoming books.
   Write soon and let me know if I converted you to being a hunter.
(joke) Keep loving those animals!

Sincerely,
Phil

"The time will come when men such as I
will look upon the murder of animals
as most now look upon the murder of men."
Leonardo da Vinci

The Hunt

My personal experiences having to do with the consideration shown to animals by some human beings are less than rewarding or warming. While researching those religions that profess that animals will receive salvation, it was impossible not to reflect on some personal, yet long suppressed animal experiences. Those painful memories of peers who unmercifully teased chained or fenced-in animals— those who would drop cats from second story heights to see if they would land on their feet-- kids that would break and tear away the shells of living turtles. Some would pull wings from flies, cut the tails off lizards, pull the claws from crayfish... and oddly enough they delighted in inflicting those wanton acts of pain and cruelty on defenseless creatures. Some acts were so brutal and pitiless that it would further injure me emotionally to relate them. Were they psychopathic or what?

Even my best friend upon receiving his driver's license delighted in running over every innocent creature that ambled onto the roadways. There were years of having to be the unfortunate bystander who witnessed farm animals suffering unbearable blows and inhumane treatment from some of their brutal, coldhearted owners. Yet those same individuals who would refuse to move a pan of water close enough to a chain-tangled, thirst-parched animal so that it could get a drink were often involved in church, 4-H, Future Farmers of America and other worthwhile community

Wherein was the real them? How could one soul possibly do that to another? Sometimes for minor offenses, a dog would be shot and when unwanted puppies or kittens were born, they were tied in gunnysacks and thrown into the pond. One of my friend's fathers enjoyed killing so much that he would hunt deer, geese and ducks, coons, rabbits, wild turkeys, squirrels, in or out of season— shoot them and walk away without looking back. If he pulled a too small fish from the water, he would toss it up on the bank rather than back into the water since it might annoy him by taking his hook the second time. Stalking the next victim was his only motivation.

My unbearable memory of this man had to do with the time he decided to teach me how to become a hunter. After spending two or more hours traipsing through the woods, we came upon a deer. P.J. grabbed my shoulder and pushed me into a crouching position. Now take careful aim and squeeze the trigger, he whispered. The roar that emitted from that weapon sounded to me like the shot heard round the world— the mother of all bombs! Upon reaching the deer, I realized the shot had only fallen, but not killed her. She laid there quivering in pain and fear. "Shoot her again," P.J. yelled.

"I can't... I can't," I nearly sobbed. The little deer looked up at me with her wondering and helpless eyes as if to ask what terrible thing had happened to her. Did I cause it? Rang out another shot that caused the world around me to go black and then for her it

128

was all over. Was stopping a bullet her only purpose in having been born?

Was this man a kill-crazed maniac? Perhaps, but he was also a fundamentalist minister... a true-blue holy roller. The words of his sermons that he screamed at the top of his lungs were like those hot balls of fire that exited the barrels of his shotgun and burned their way into the muscle and bone of his animal victims. Many were the poverty-stricken members of his small Ozark mountain church who could have benefited from the meat or the fur those animals would have provided, but his obsession was the kill. Any compassion or understanding in having hands to help others didn't seem to be within the figments of his understanding. His animal victims were left to die and rot. Was this man a devil in human form? Was he the proverbial wolf dressed in the sheep's clothing? Did not Peter write that the devil is the one who walks about seeking that which he can devour? Hawthorne once asked what other dungeon could be so dark as one's own heart.

> "He that slayeth an ox is as he that killeth a man."
> **Isaiah**

Cats and far too many hunters alike, both kill not because they're hungry, but for sport. 50% of deer struck by arrows are never recovered and are left to die an excruciatingly painful and agonizing death.

[Most of the statistical information provided at this time comes from the ASPCA, American Humane Association, Animal Rights Online, Animal Angels

Ben Garwood

Anonymous, Wild and Wonderful Wildlife, as well as numerous similar organizations.]

"Wild animals never kill for sport.
Man is the only one to whom the torture and death
Of his fellow creatures is amusing in itself."
James A. Froude 1818-1894

Need some more statistics? In the U.S. every year, all totaled up— five to nine billion animals of which staggering numbers were raised under unspeakable and torturous conditions are commercially slaughtered for food. That represents nearly two animals for every person on earth— per year! Half of the country's fresh water supply goes to these unfortunate animals, not just for their thirst needs, but for countless other things such as washing down the slaughterhouse floors. That same industry requires one third of our fossil fuel for such things as refrigeration, freezing, cooking (as with processed lunch meats, etc.) and transportation to markets... just for starters. By this end of this century, 650 species of animals will have become extinct.

"As long as there are slaughterhouses
there will be battlefields."
Leo Tolstoy

Unicorns & More

The author of creation must have loved his creatures, for in the 39th chapter of Job that speaks of animals, it is stated how the Lord made the wilderness to house the wild ass, and the barren land to be his place of dwelling. The unicorn is mentioned in that chapter as well as in many previously stated scriptures.

Oh, you still thought the unicorn was but a myth— an animal of fables? Well, it was, but you know how it goes— someone told someone who told someone who told Job... so what the heck? Would it come as a surprise to learn that many respectable, notable, and reputable persons personally made claim to having seen the unicorn— that horse with a single horn? That list would include Aristotle, and Julius Caesar among many others.

Do you find interest in all the varieties of fish, and do you take pleasure in watching them swim about in their unique aquatic environments?

And of course the Bible mentions a great fish that was said to have once swallowed a man named Jonah. Job refers to one great fish as being a leviathan. Could that fish have been what we call a whale? I can still hear my Sunday school teacher singing, "The fish swam up, mouth open wide, and did swallow old Jonah cause otherwise he'd died."

Have you observed the gracefulness of a deer or the stealth of a fox? Have you been to the zoo and been surprised to see the many ways that some of the primates are just like us? Have you watched the mothers of the large cat families tending to their young? Do you know that some mammals live in the water? Do you enjoy the chipmunks, the squirrels, the rabbits, the opossums and raccoon that might live right in your own neighborhood?

And just how many animals are there? Well, there's at least 200,000 species of fur bearing or feathered animals, not to mention 800,000 varieties of insects— and not all bugs are insects, you know. A friend of mine who was a science teacher once told his students that it would take 7,000 pages in small print just to list the scientific names of all those little six-legged animals we call insects. So we know there are many, many kinds of animals— but every year about 10,000 new ones are discovered and some scientists say there may be as many as ten million we don't yet know about.

Do you have hands of love to help at least some of those animals? Are you aware of their biological needs? Do you regularly place food and water within their reach? Are you aware of their sighs and sorrows? Are you there for them in their times of need? Do you know that animals of all sizes and shapes have many of the same requirements for life that you do? Do you know that animals endure the same emotions as people? Animals often become stressed and depressed. Because they are alone and cannot ask for help, they often become bewildered and disoriented. Often times it is impossible for them to find food or water and for those two reasons alone, many of them perish.

Consider how much you might miss animals if suddenly all animals were to be no more. The gorilla and elephant populations, as well as many other well-known species, are dwindling at alarming rates. Gorillas are killed so that their hands can be lacquered and used as ashtrays. Elephants are slaughtered for their ivory tusks. (Remember that by the end of this century, 650 more species of animals will have become extinct.) Every year, up to nine billion animals are slaughtered for food while two hundred million more are sacrificed to cosmetic and medical research. Countless billions freeze to death and die from a lack of food and water— die in forest fires or from being run over on the highways. And the slaughter of animals by hunters and trappers brings about the death of even more millions.

"Though this may be play to you, 'Tis death to us."
Aesop

Are They Really Dumb Beasts?

Since the Biblical days, animal devotees and scientists have proven over and again that many species of animals have demonstrated not only an ability to understand and respond to human language, but also to accomplish incredibly complex tasks. Some animals are even smart enough to lie— such as mother birds when they fake wing injuries to draw danger away from the nest. Others will fly to a distant place and create a vocal disturbance while successfully encouraging other birds to join them in their efforts to deceive. There are male monkeys who attract females by uttering the sound for "food" to draw them near— even when no food is present.

Not only can they *parrot* human words and count, some parrots can master complex intellectual concepts better than some children under the age of five, and other parrots can name 50 different objects and count them in groups of eight. There are dogs that can navigate mazes with more skill than humans. Animals experience shame and know to fear retribution for improper behavior. Animals also have the capacity to express regret— ask forgiveness and seek understanding.

Be honest! Do you ever talk to your pet as if it could actually understand what you're saying? Do you ask questions as if it could really answer? What if it mentally can but physically can't? What if the *animal* is capable of communicating thought but you are not? Thornton Wilder said: "The best thing about animals is that they don't talk too much." Well, a true animal devotee might not agree with that. Even those of us who profess no psychic ability, but who know and understand animals, realize that our animals are communicating with us all the time. We learn to read their expressions— to sense their very movements and read their emotions.

Scientists have successfully enabled some of the primates to type words while others are being successfully taught to play video games. Raccoons and opossums, which do not make good house pets, have the mental capacity to train themselves to litter boxes in a matter of hours... sometimes in less time than a domestic animal. In fact, some scientists tell us that human and chimpanzee brains are so remarkably similar in circuitry, that the genes of the two species are 98.4% identical.

But it's not just the chimpanzees that are so smart— for some scientists and animal researchers believe pigs to be among the smartest of all members of the animal kingdom. Indeed a friend of ours, "Peggy June Raccoon," has trained her potbellied pig to respond to verbal commands such as *roll over, beg, sit, lay down...* just like a dog!

Winston Churchill, an animal lover, made an interesting observation about pigs, noting that as dogs looked up to us humans, cats looked down at us, but pigs accepted us as equals. How empty must be the hearts of those who consider an animal to be nothing more than a dumb beast. If some of their brains were put into birds, the poor things would probably try to fly

Ben Garwood

backwards. Was it Mark Twain who once offered that analogy?

Since we are capable of loving animals and they are capable of loving us back, is that not another indication that we might be spiritual soul mates? Any animal rehabilitator will recall persons having rescued an injured animal who ask if they can have it back when its injuries have healed. You see- they love it so much they yearn to keep it for their own and share life with it. It then becomes necessary to explain that the greatest love of all is to let it return to the calling of its own nature.

"Freedom is that faculty which
enlarges the usefulness of all other faculties."
Kant

All Brawn & No Brain?

Nearly a century ago, a man by the name of George Humphrey examined the animal known as the jellyfish. What could be less significant than some animal that exists in stagnant water and has no eyes with which to see? Yet, while closely examining what many persons would have considered to be among the most insignificant of all animals, Humphrey noted the most amazing findings. For example, this blob of jelly, with no brain or internal organs whatever (just a bit higher in rank than an amoeba), is capable of moving about of its own resolve. Some jellyfish have tentacles up to thirty inches long while others extend to six feet. Bodies can range from one to sixteen inches and the *sting* of some can be fatal even after the animal is dead. Insignificant creatures? What is most surprising is that this animal has no mind. How could it? If there be no brain— where would the mind be located?

Consider these inquiries: Does not everything require a location? Does a soul have a location? What if— the soul hovers near but apart from the body— like a halo? What if it communicates with us from some distant place? After all, some psychics claim that such detached message interaction is possible. Perhaps in the dimension wherein a soul might exist... distance does not exist? Could a soul intercede for a brain in a lower life form until an evolutionary process creates what we might call a spiritual intellect?

137

Ben Garwood

Well, the jellyfish must have some aura of intelligence, for it likes darkness, and when light falls upon it— it moves away. What is telling it to move and to respond to outside stimuli? It can readily determine preferable resting places and is drawn to what it thus considers to be a pleasant environment. Since it has no mouth, one might wonder— how does it eat? Since it has no stomach— where does the food go? Let's answer the question: *How does it eat?* Therein is a very unique answer. The jellyfish encloses the available food source with its body or a body part and consumes it by more or less absorbing it. Matters not which part of the jellyfish comes into contact with the food— let's call it osmosis.

"Maybe the Lord just didn't want us to know about everything all at once.
After all, without a mystery here and there, life would be pretty boring."
Samuel Martin

Consider those animals called sponges— once believed to have been plants of which there are 15,000 different species. No internal organs! Insignificant? Hang on tight... for it is possible that those animals will populate the ocean longer than mankind will populate the earth!

Could that osmosis process of the jellyfish and sponge in any way be related to the way the spirit has been absorbed by any animal body or vice-versa? Could it be that a soul precedes the brain and that it is only later in the evolutionary process when the *soul bone connecta to de brain bone?*

138

Aside from the five known senses, could that process be analogous to the spirit of a sixth sense moving within us? Must we, or animals, have a body organ for every function— especially one that is pious? Is that another of the silly rules? Since we're both animals, could not the human soul, or spirit, be somehow related to the invisible intellect of the jellyfish? Instead of a body without organisms— how about yet to be defined (call them spiritual) organisms without a body? Intelligence/intellect with no enclosure. Just because something cannot be seen nor scientifically identified— does that mean it cannot exist? After all, not long ago the world's most highly respected medical authorities denied the existence of germs. Be sure of this— not religion nor science has yet even cracked the light to all that is to one day be known— and just because it can't be proven now, doesn't mean it won't be common knowledge and accepted fact by the time the next page is turned.

"Inventors and men of genius have always at first been regarded as fools..."
Dostoevsky 19th c.

One little, two little three little senses... four little five little six little senses... is there a sixth sense? That entity is believed by some to be a divine gift of the psychics. If so, is the gift more highly developed in some of us than in others? And is it a gift or a curse? Could there be a seventh or eighth sense? Truth be known, there might be many senses yet to be discovered and perhaps even mental capabilities beyond what we presently limit to senses. Yes— it is highly possible and even probable that we have those (extra) sensory perceptions that reach well beyond the primitive body functions of sight, smell, taste, touch, and hearing. Could one of those senses be the driving force that has motivated, if not obsessed, vast numbers of the human race from even the ancient times to seek a greater power? It should be stated that many researchers have entertained the notion that at least some animals might have a sense beyond us humans. What is an instinct? Could instinct be the voice of a guardian angel? Later. Meantime know that Emerson advised trusting an instinct to the end.

Are there *clues*, if we are receptive, that can lead us to knowledge that will increase our existing powers? Is this not what the modern day witches proclaim? The simple way out would be to excuse our inquisitive nature from any further pursuit of this area under discussion. Yet, should we blindly dismiss everything we might consider to be evil, mythical, superstitious, and imaginative? What if Edison had listened to his contenders and given-up on his imaginings that he, a mere man, could place light into darkness? What if Marconi had submitted to the ridicule of his antagonists and abandoned his determination to send sound across invisible waves?

Is it possible that psychic phenomenon is likewise real-- telepathy or extra sensory perception included? Is it that much less impossible than a radio wave? What about the premonitions, hunches, omens, or signs that some claim to perceive? Just because you or I can't do it doesn't mean it can't be done! Is there anything whatever to fears or haunting suspicions... autosuggestions? Just how much does hypnosis have to offer?

So what about "instincts?" When all else fails us, what have we left other than instincts? To what extent is intellect, self-preservation and instinct shared by animals and humans? If such a sense or instinct does exist, could it not be common to animals and humans alike? If any creature has instinct or potential enough to appreciate this life's existence to the extent that it makes a mental and physical effort to protect itself from harm, would not that creature, especially, be found deserving of its creator's eternal protective blessing? If that creature had intelligence enough to wish to remain a conscious entity in this life, would it not wish to do so in an existence of another dimension yet to follow?

Is there any good reason, scientific or spiritual, why even an insect should not have lasting consciousness? And can it be possible that even though as animal *beings,* the man and the jellyfish are equal to nature's overall diagram? Even if the man is a bit more equal, in no way does that suggest the jellyfish is insignificant.

Consider that Goethe said, "Even the flowers of life are but illusions."
What if it turns out that nothing does exist except in the mind of God? Could it be that there is no substance— that nothing is material? If so, then we exist only in a state of virtual reality. If

141

Ben Garwood

God ceases to keep us in his thoughts, do we cease to exist?

Enroute

There are, of course, many speculations and visions as to where an animal heaven could be, what it might be like, and what the journey to that pie in the sky would entail. From childhood comes the memory of a sermon-story by a much-admired Methodist minister, an Ozark mountain man who has long been tenderly remembered. As best his sermon can be recalled, there were two streams coming from different origins. One day they joined as one, and as their singularity began they spoke to one another. One very healthy looking stream asked what appeared to be a less-fortunate stream what its journey had been like, to which came the reply that it was horrible. That stream's journey had been chemically polluted and consisted of struggling through mucky swamps and pools of stagnant waters.

And then that stream asked of the other stream, 'How was your journey?' And that stream answered, "Mine was a delightful path that trickled through moss-covered rocks and well-vegetated banks from whereupon came ripples of warm life-giving sunshine. I am sad that your journey was not as fortunate. What a pity that yours was not a happy one."

And it was then when the two streams now flowing together merged with a mighty river which spoke to them with a loud voice saying: "Flow into me and dismiss whatever the memories of your journeys for soon we will enter a new existence as we return to our mother, the sea."

It was many years later in my literary discovery of, *The Wanderer,* [The River] by Kahlil Gibran, when I realized from where the minister might have taken his sermon. Doubtful if any two readers would interpret Gibran's writings or the Reverend's sermon in the same way, but of course the streams philosophically represented the spiritual journeys of two separate individuals. How that little story cannot help but refresh the recall of one who said, *"Come unto me, those of you who are heavy laden, and I will give you rest."*

Is there a proven way to get to heaven?

A

Yes. Turn right and go straight.

"As there is a special place for all the souls of men according to their number, so is there also of the beasts."
Enoch LV111-5

The Arlington Pet Cemetery Rockford, Illinois

For some time now, Mary and I have worked as volunteers for the Arlington Pet Cemetery. Mostly our labors and contributions have consisted of landscaping and gardening. Our favorite creation therein is known as Rainbow Ridge— the name of that garden having been adapted from the poem of the similar name, Rainbow Bridge.

"There is a bridge connecting heaven and earth. It is called the Rainbow Bridge because of its many colors. Just this side of the Rainbow Bridge there is a land of meadows, hills, and valleys with lush green grass. When a beloved pet dies, the pet goes to this place. There is always food, water, and warm spring weather. The old and frail animals are young again. Those who are maimed are made whole again. They play all day with one another. There is only one thing missing. They are not with their special person who loved them on earth. So, each day they run and play until the day comes when one suddenly stops playing and looks up. The nose twitches! The ears are up! The eyes are staring! And then one suddenly runs from the group. You have been seen, and when you and your special friend meet, you take him or her again in your arms and embrace. Your face is kissed again and again and again, and you look once more into the eyes of your trusting pet. Then you cross Rainbow Bridge together, never again to be

Ben Garwood

separated."

--author unknown--

A woman who has two dogs buried at Arlington brought a copy of the following wonderful eulogy to the cemetery last summer. It is a very famous animal speech once offered by George Graham Vest during a courtroom hearing in 1870. Mr. Vest later served more than two decades in the U.S. Senate. His speech to follow is now recorded in the *Congressional Record* and is called: "Eulogy on the Dog:"

Gentleman of the jury, the best friend a man has in this world may turn against him and become his enemy. His son or daughter whom he has reared with loving care may prove ungrateful. Those who are nearest and dearest to us— those whom we trust with our happiness and our good name— may become traitors to their faith. The money that a man has he may lose. It flies away from him, perhaps when he needs it most. A man's reputation may be sacrificed in a moment of ill-considered action. The people who are prone to fall on their knees to do us honor when success is with us may be the first to throw the stone of malice when failure settles its cloud upon our heads. The one absolute, unselfish friend that man can have in this selfish world— the one that never deserts him, the one that never proves ungrateful or treacherous— is his dog.

Gentlemen of the jury, a man's dog stands by him in prosperity and in poverty, in health and in sickness. He will sleep on the cold ground, where the wintry winds blow and the snow drives fiercely, if only he can be near his master's side. He will kiss the hand that has no food to offer, he will lick the wounds and sores that come in encounter with the roughness of the world. He guards the sleep of his pauper master as if he were a prince. When all other friends desert, he remains. When riches take wings and reputation falls to pieces he is as constant in his

146

love as the sun in its journey through the heavens. If fortune drives the master forth an outcast in the world, friendless and homeless, the faithful dog asks no privilege other than that of accompanying him to guard against danger, to fight against his enemies. And when the last scene of all comes, and death takes the master in its embrace, and his body is laid away in the cold ground, no matter if all other friends pursue their way, there by his graveside will the noble dog be found, his head between his paws, his eyes sad but open in alert and watchfulness, faithful and true even to death.

Perhaps some persons who have never felt the warmth of animal love could not hope to understand the stalwart bond that frequently exists between animal and person, but in the Arlington burial ground of the once living animal— the very headstones call forth with devotion that will never fade away. Here are just a few of the headstone epitaphs: *He Was a Good Little Doggie Boy ~ In Our Hearts Forever ~ History's Finest Greyhound ~ You Brought Joy To Our Hearts ~ Journeyed Home ~ We Love and Miss You ~ In Life the Firmest Friends, First to Welcome, Foremost to Defend.*

"The great pleasure of a dog is that if you make a fool of yourself not only will he not scold you, but will make a fool of himself, too."

Samuel Butler

At the Arlington Animal Cemetery, it is not uncommon for an entire family to attend the burial service of their beloved pet, and occasionally a minister friend will accompany the bereaved in their meaningful farewell. And why not include that historical representative *voice from the wilderness?*

147

As of Genesis to Malachi [Old Testament]...from Matthew to Revelations [New Testament]... animals of a hundred-fold are mentioned in the scriptures. Bible verse after Bible verse talks of the oxen, camels, and donkeys— the sheep and horses, and one cannot help but relive the bond and appreciation that once existed between animal and master.

Once upon a time, a stranger to the Arlington Pet cemetery approached Mary and me and asked how it could be that there were persons who placed so much emphasis on their deceased animals. "Why would they purchase exclusive gravesites, coffins, and stones... just for a dead animal?" Little did he realize how many persons had shared their feelings that their animals were as important to them as their children. Some would quietly admit that whereas their offspring had sorely mistreated them, their animals remained faithful to the end. And little did this visitor realize the hopes of those looking forward to be rejoined with their animals in what they are determined will be another dimension to come.

Now this man wasn't a meanie or anything like that. He was a gentleman, an individual of values and his questions were sincere, but his final response was: "Well they won't be together again. Animals don't have souls so they can't go to heaven."

He shouldn't be too sure of that— and too bad he couldn't have talked with Will Rogers. My dad who once met Will and was one of his biggest fans, said Will wrote in his own autobiography that when believing in something having to do with another world, not to get too hung up on insisting what it's going to be like. That way you won't start out there all disappointed. Will Rogers certainly must have loved animals, for Dad remembered that Will having once said if dogs don't go to heaven, he wanted to go where the dogs went.

Still another man visited the cemetery one day whom we both knew to be a devout Christian. He too, did not believe that animals could go to heaven, yet he had a dog buried in the animal cemetery and paid his respects on a regular basis. One can only hope he will rejoice like the Shepard who found his sheep when one day he crosses Rainbow Bridge and finds his beloved friend waiting there for him. There will be many surprises in heaven's name.

"Every beast of the forest is mine, and the cattle upon a thousand hills.
I know all the fowls of the mountains, and the wild beasts of the field are mine."
Psalms 50: 10,11
"And I saw heaven opened, and behold a white horse and he that sat upon him was called Faithful and True."
Revelation 19:2
"Seeing, they see not, and hearing they hear not, neither do they understand."
Bible

Rejoice, I Have Found My Sheep

So are the animals important to God? In the Christian religion, Christ is portrayed as the Good Shepherd, the keeper of the sheep. One has but to recall the verse of that glorious hymn, *The Ninety and Nine* [edited and paraphrased here] to know the love of a Shepherd for his sheep:

Ninety and Nine safely lay in the shelter of the fold, but one was lost in the hills away, far from the gates of gold. The shepherd had there his ninety and nine, were they not enough for him? No. One of the flock had gone astray. The path was rough, and the path was steep, but he went to the desert to find his sheep. Still those protected never knew how deep were those waters crossed, nor how dark was the night that the shepherd passed through, ere he found his sheep that was lost. Then out in the dessert he heard its cry— sick and helpless and ready to die. And those blood drops marking the mountain track? Shed for one who had gone astray, so the shepherd could bring him back. And then from the mountains thunder driven, and up from the rocky steep, there rose a glad cry to the gate of heaven, "Rejoice I have found my sheep."

•••

"What man of you, having a hundred sheep, if he lose one of them, doth not leave the ninety and nine and go after that which is lost, until he finds it? And would he not then say, Rejoice with me for I have found my sheep which was lost?"
Luke 15:4

What did the dragon ask after he ate the flock of sacrificial lambs?

Why do I feel so sheepish?

True, the ninety and nine was a parable-like sonnet, which depicted a human being caught-up in sin, but the bottom line is a reminder that the Lord does not exclude even a single identity. The Lord brings back his own. Surely after heaven and earth have passed away, the Lord will call back his animals for they too, number among his flock. Salvation, however defined, is a gift from the giver of life alone.

It is true that even the angels in heaven are said to rejoice upon the salvation of one single human soul. In fact, scripture [Luke 15:7] says, "I say unto you, that likewise joy shall be in heaven over one sinner that repenteth, more than ninety and nine just persons, which need no repentance." How very touching. Why then would they not *weep*, for the rest of eternity, upon witnessing the permanent demise of *descillions* of billions of animals? The only thing ever comparable to that would have been the fall of the angels!

Was it perhaps the *Tibetan Book of the Dead,* from whence these words in italics were jotted on paper to be used in my classroom? Not sure. *"As a man's desire is, so is his destiny. For as his desire, so is his*

151

will. And as his will is, so is his deed, and as his deed is, so is his reward, whether good or bad." And yes, the Tibetans believed animals to have souls.

For many of us, our desire to do good not only encloses, but reaches beyond the acts of benevolence we can extend to our fellow humankind. Our love also broadens to the other variety (animals) with which we share this world of our universe. Could there be anything more important than our sharing of talent and compassion? People often ask those who give so unselfishly of themselves to others— why they are willing to do so while receiving nothing in return? Nothing in return? Must everything be measured by monetary compensation? What greater realization could any human have beyond knowing we can't take it with us but we can send it on ahead?

"To have and not give is often worse than to steal."
Marie von Ebner Eschenbach - 1893

We go where we are attached, so if our heaven is within us, we create our own destiny. What greater opportunity to be of service to mankind than to merge our past and our present to help shape the future? Even if some of our garden might have been infested with thorns, we can still send our roses on ahead. After all, we can't take anything with us— so why not send it on ahead? It is truly more blessed to give than to receive!

We then, are like the Good Shepherd. It is a blessing when it becomes our will and opportunity to care enough about the lost sheep whether human or

152

animal to return it to the fold. That the grace of God might shine on any being forever should be our desire and we should do everything possible to make it the destiny. And just because we can't see the final destiny? Then we must rely upon those things we can see to give us faith for those things we cannot see.

"Faith is the substance of things hoped for and the evidence of things unseen."
Hebrews 11:11

Do Animals Go To Heaven?

How can we possibly conclude any answer to that lingering question? "Do animals go to heaven?" Well, for those who have eyes to see and ears to hear, and are capable of being enlightened by the spirit, methinks we already established that fact. But when we do approach the Christian religion as a source to substantiate that answer, we should consider that Jesus said he came to this world not for the whole, but for those who were sick and in need of a physician. Since the animals were not sick by that assumed spiritual definition, why would Christ have taken time from his short visit to detail their eternity? Jesus didn't come here to bring salvation to animals—so there is no reason for scripture that focuses on the mission and objectives of Christ to address that subject any more than extraterrestrial life.

Common sense would suggest that if animals go to heaven, they were already guaranteed salvation—from the very moment of their conception. Beyond that they weren't part of the equation. That possibility of pre-destination certainly sounds reasonable. Should one wish to learn about classic literature, they wouldn't seek such knowledge in an algebra text. The Bible is a human text and since we don't have an animal text, we must read between the lines and allow the spirit to guide us to the hidden truths wherein the answer to our question can be found.

According to Christian doctrine, human beings have what is known as free will, yet nothing Biblical whatever indicates an entitlement of free will referring to animals. What? Not even for cats...? Nope. Not even for "Fat Cats!" And what's more, there's no Ten Commandments for the animals. Therefore, as free will can be related to sin, animals are incapable of sin. That does not suggest they are incapable of wrongdoing— just ask any carpet installer, but they are incapable of Biblically defined sin. It's hard for many to believe that animals are not already entitled to pre-destined squatters rights within the Pearly Gates. Keep those alternative rules of the road in mind. God does have the right to endow them with implied domain, doesn't he?

Within the personal experiences of most persons, no one among their friends has ever visited heaven and come back to talk about it. Therefore, might it dare be said, no one really knows much of anything about heaven? Samuel Martin said if there are no vices whatever, it would sure be a pretty boring place unless the animals are there. Still~ if animals do not go to the people heaven, short of reincarnation, what would be the alternatives? There are at least three: hell, a state of non-existence, or an animal heaven. To many persons, either of the first two options would represent cruel and unusual punishment and hardly a behavior representative of a God whose love is said to exceed all of man's understanding.

I personally, have several friends belonging to belief systems other than my own— who with tears in their eyes assure me there can be no eternal life for me unless I convert to their belief. Considering there

155

are so many religions professing to be the only true religion and believing hell or annihilation awaits those who don't think according to their guidelines— it's certainly understandable that they might believe animals can't go to heaven.

**Why is it that persons entering heaven are asked to remain silent
until reaching their final destinations?**

A

So as not to draw attention to themselves since some of the populace thinks they're the only ones who were accepted.

"Histories are more filled with the fidelity of dogs than of friends."
Alexander Pope 1688-1744

Thank goodness, for heaven's sake, that it is not a sin to at least hope that animals can go to heaven, and that allowing one's child to share that hope is not the same as attempting to keep them believing in Santa Claus until they're old enough to vote. To all existing knowledge, there is no diagnosed disorder that results from entertaining the possibility of having our pets join us on the other side of River Jordan.

"Seems to me that if we couldn't establish identification by the shapes of their bodies,
that when it comes to some,
we might not be able to tell which is the human and which is the animal."

"In God's hand is the soul of every living thing."
Job 12:10

Ben & Pooch

Those who have read Mary's *Pawprints Upon My Heart* will recall the very touching story of "Ben and Pooch," the tale of what Mary called *The Saddest Story Ever Told.* It was about me and an orphaned hound dog puppy our family picked-up along the roadside while returning from church one Sunday, and the circumstances under which we were parted.

Before the day was over, Pooch was clearly "Ben's boy," and although 56 years have now elapsed since the beginning of that friendship, it seems like it was only yesterday. Since the entire story can be read in Mary's book, I will only brief the details:

At the time Poochie entered my life, my father was a hardworking, industrious businessman who was the manager of a J.J. Newberry chain store. We enjoyed a solid middle class life and resided in a semi-rural and heavily forested neighborhood with hills and a creek. Everything a boy and his dog could ask for.

Even before that time, I can remember Father telling me that one of the most important things to learn is that *life is not always fair.* Doubtful at that time I could have realized how soon our family would be experiencing the truth in that adage. By the time Pooch was two years old, Father had resigned his position with the chain store hoping to excel as an entrepreneur in his own business. Unfortunately, this meant leaving the wonderful abode of #2 Sherwood Forest in Belleville, Illinois and moving to 4047 Magnolia Place and the heavily congested streets of St. Louis, Missouri.

Although the beautiful Magnolia Park with its ponds and spectacular landscaping was but a half-block away, it could not begin to replace Sherwood Forest. Not for me and not for Pooch. I would spent hours riding the streets of St. Louis on my "Green Hornet," Montgomery Ward bicycle. Pooch, tongue hanging out of his mouth, would be panting alongside every mile of the way. Clear down to the Mississippi River to watch the barges and the big Riverboat, the Admiral. When weather didn't permit *travel,* I would practice the piano and my drum and bugle corps bugle. Pooch would *sing along* to all my musical efforts.

I guess it's just impossible for parents to realize how deep a bonding can take place between a boy and his dog— especially when that boy was being physically and psychologically bullied every day at school— and had no friends other than his faithful "Poochie." They couldn't have known, because otherwise they would never have decided St. Louis was no place for a big dog like Pooch and sent him off to the dog pound.

The day I was required to place Pooch in the back of the "dog catchers truck" was the truly the saddest day of my life up to this time. My heart was ripped to shreds as we looked into one another's eyes for the very last time. That torn heart has not mended since— nor will it ever.

There is an adage that says:
"The sky is not less blue because the blind man cannot see it."

What was equally as painful for my father was that his business failed and a short time thereafter he was required to move his family from the perks and advantages of city life to the Ozark Mountains. How Pooch would have loved those big hills.

I never knew what became of Pooch, but dogs by the hundreds rendered themselves a nuisance to the neighborhoods of St. Louis, so I hold no hope that Pooch long survived his destination.

Upon reaching our new community, we joined a somewhat fundamental *church in the wildwood.* I really liked the new life and made many friends. The preacher, who was the embodiment of a mountain man in every way, became one of my favorite persons. Then one day, while thinking of Pooch, I asked him: "Do dogs go to heaven? When the gentle giant explained to me that it was only people and not animals that could go to heaven— the not yet healed wounds in my heart were ripped asunder once again.

The pillow beneath my head was moist with tears that night as I asked God, "Why not? Why couldn't you let animals into heaven?

"By night on my bed I sought him whom my soul loveth;
I sought him, but I found him not."
Solomon's Song 3:1

Following that second sorrowful experience having

159

to do with Pooch, I scribbled some words that could be sung to the folk song Danny Boy in his memory. I possibly borrowed or edited some of the original script— since seventh grade it's too many years to remember, but the emotion is there nonetheless. In spite of what the preacher would have me believe, I was as convinced then as I am today that I would one day be with Pooch again:

POOCHIE BOY
Oh, Poochie Boy, the bugle's still a-calling
From where I be to Sherwood Forest's side

Our fun times gone, and both our hearts left crying
T'was you that went, though here I still abide.

But come us back when born again forever
When timelessness will bond us once again
Yes we'll be there, with life that leaves us never
Oh, Poochie Boy, my priceless treasured friend.

And when time comes, when all we know has severed
Since we were dead, as dead we surely be
We'll find that place where once we spent together
And run and play again just you and me.

And though I'll sleep, where soft you'll soon tread over me
It's then my grave will warmer, sweeter be,
For you will whine and tell me that you love me
And I will wake that day I know you'll come to me.

And now? Well I do my best to heed the advice I give to others in order to cope with the loss of their animals. I reassure myself that the three or four years Pooch and I spent together surely must have contributed a happiness to his life that he would never have otherwise known and spared him from an even earlier demise.

"A true friend is one soul in two bodies."
Aristotle

Tony

Although Tony belonged to another man, who was like a surrogate father to me, that kind-hearted individual had for all practical purposes let Tony be my horse. I got to share weekends with Tony as well endless days during the summer months.

Tony was a young and beautiful quarter horse— whose primary function in life was that of a cow pony. So skilled was Tony in understanding his responsibility, that his rider could drape the reins around the saddle horn and Tony would bring all 36 head of cattle to the barnyard by himself.

Countless were the times that Tony and I would journey off into the hills and bluffs— cross the streams and rivers and enjoy the wonders of nature together. I say "together" because Tony seemed to find pleasure in every step of the way. Although Tony had never been put to a plow, he often assisted in pulling stumps and in the wintertime a sled of logs to be cut-up into firewood. I would make frequent trips to town on him bringing back supplies in the saddle bags. Truly, here was the city boy turned mountain boy. That portion of my life still remains the greatest single experience of my youth, and Tony was very much a part of it.

Tony and I shared one another's lives for about six years. Then one Saturday morning as I arrived at the farm, I noticed Tony was not standing in his usual place. It was predictable enough that when I would be coming, that as often as not— Tony would be waiting for me. Even after pulling the car up to the barnyard, Tony was not to be seen.

I whistled, I called. The other horses responded, but no Tony. And then I saw a dark form laying on the ground by the far gate. I ran as fast as I could— and there laid Tony... the ground soaked in his own blood. Someone had shot him in the head.

Had hunters mistaken him for a deer? Not likely. Had a stray bullet hit him? Not likely. Tony would often walk to the far side of the pasture—seemingly to watch the cars, tractors, and other teams pass by on the old dirt road. There were other passersby—kids for example, who would ride in the back of pick-up trucks and shoot rabbits—sometimes stray dogs. Somehow, I knew it was them who had shot Tony... on purpose— and later learned that my suspicions were true.

Wounded and badly bleeding, Tony headed for the barnyard but it was to be another day or two before anyone would be there. He succeeded in reaching the only destination he knew where help might be found, while there and alone, he passed on to that unknown dimension.

Tony unwillingly forfeited one of life's greatest gifts— that of growing old. Sometimes people ask me what it's like to be growing older. I don't know, but thus far every new day is a blessing beyond yesterday. Unless we are suffering from a physical or mental disability— I wonder if many persons even realize they are growing older. Even though I am beyond the 65 mile mark, my spirit is still that of a teenager. I feel like I could still jump on Tony's back and let him run like the wind— carrying me across the fields of clover and wheat. I feel like Pooch and I could still sprint up and down the hills of Sherwood Forest or successfully dodge the streetcars and ice cream vendors on the busy streets of St. Louis.

Old Samuel Martin once told me there's no age possible to the spirit and that because of that we'd best be acting like we thought others of our age should be acting. Well, perhaps some of us just refuse to *grow up...* but what if, aside from this carcass that presently carries us about, we truly are *ageless*?

Kids, especially, ask if I fear death. Of course that's understandable since they likely perceive me to be a hundred and fifty years old and ready to schedule an appointment with the grim reaper. Proof of that is found in the fact that they always believe me when I tell them I was in the Civil War. I assure them that I do not fear death. In fact, I am in some ways looking forward to it. You see, there will be at least thirty of my animal friends waiting for me at the Rainbow Ridge.

"Should auld acquaintance be forgot and never brought to mind?"
Auld Lang Syne (Burns)

Nice To Come Home To

Many persons say that if it were not for their animal to come home to after work, they would be unable to face the next day. There are those who claim the whole of their existence is to share life with and provide for their pet. Harboring that notion, according to some, would be indicative of a person in need of mental health therapy. Know what? Such persons who share companionship with an animal and at least have a pet to cling to are receiving therapy— and such a lifestyle is (usually) a given choice. Wouldn't even a dog or a cat be a more suitable and pleasant companion that an incompatible spouse or a cantankerous roommate?

Believe it. Those animal lovers are functioning— they are producing. For them to profess their animal is foremost in their lives does not spell mental illness. Should we all send off for one of those mail-order degrees in psychology before expostulating any further on that hypothesis? There are many who say they believe that until one has shared love between and betwixt an animal, there is a portion of the (human) soul that has never fully developed. Remember Ebenezer Elliot saying if it were not for his cat and dog he thought he could not live?

A (true) story often passed around between animal lovers tells of a young girl saddened by the loss of her dog being personally comforted by Martin Luther who offered his assurances that her dog would go to heaven. Luther is also credited with having said that in the *new heavens and the new earth, all creatures will not only be harmless, but lovely and joyful.* Luther fully believed that both animal and man came from not only the breath, but the spirit of God. As for Martin Luther, he left us with no questions regarding his conviction that animals do have souls and will go to heaven. He, like St. Francis, was an animal advocate in the fullest sense of the word.

Another account having to do with Luther tells of his chastising some hunters— telling them that as they pursued the animal, they reminded him of the devil pursing human souls. Although Luther was a superstitious person, he was an extraordinary genius in other ways. Not only was he a former Catholic Priest, a musician, and the leader of the Reformation, but when he translated the Bible into German, he helped to create the modern German language. Shall we assume that the founder of the Protestant religion might have had some insight as to whether animals can go to heaven? Can any of the doubters demonstrate genius comparable to that of Luther?

"Maid of Athens, ere we part, Give, oh, give me back my heart!
Byron

SOUR GRAPES

As has already been mentioned, after Mary's book, *Pawprints Upon My Heart* was published, she was soon to be frequented with the question, "Can animals go to heaven?" Following her redirecting one such question to me, I replied to the pre-teen girl that it was my personal belief animals would go to heaven. A day later the young lady brought me a hand-written, anger-filled-response. It was from her minister, stating among other things that animals did not have souls and therefore could not go to heaven. Here is a portion of that letter.

"Animals do not beleive in Jesus and canot be baptised or take comunion. They are not born of water and canot be born again. They do not have souls and they canot seek repenitance and canot go to heven!"

Repentance from what? Did they forget to keep the Sabbath Holy? Exodus 20:10 certainly defined the Sabbath day to include animals so that they could rest, too. Did one raccoon covet the hollow tree another raccoon had claimed as its own? Did a hawk swoop down and murder a field mouse?

> "Most of the shadows in this life are caused
> by standing in one's own sunshine."
> **Ralph Waldo Emerson**

His letter was quite lengthy and filled with

167

misspelled sermon-like text. Perhaps he never heard those words of wisdom that say one should be careful when giving another a piece of their mind that they still have enough left to get by the rest of the day. Anyway how then was it that anyone being so thorough could have missed the part in Matthew 18:3 that says unless ye be converted and come to me as little children, ye shall not enter the kingdom of heaven? Well, couldn't dogs be put on rewind and go back to puppies? Surprising also that he didn't quote 2 Peter 3:14 where it is written that we will be without 'spot' in heaven. When he spoke of being born by water, was he speaking of baptism or evolution? Let me try to guess. Wonder if he knows that Jesus never baptized anybody.

He assured me my soul was in danger of hell fire and that I should be looking for *signs* so as to repent while there was still time. What?!? Because I believe animals can go to heaven? Besides, Jesus said it is an evil and adulterous generation that seeks signs and that there shall be no signs... but wait— didn't Isaiah 66:19 say, "I will set a sign among them?" Maybe he was referring to the sign that says turn right and go straight?

See how easy it is to get confused? Anyway, shame on me for any vilification directed toward that minister. He was only following his conscience and his belief system. Abraham Lincoln did say it is better to remain silent and be thought a fool than to speak out and remove all doubt, so perhaps he and I both should just keep our mouths shut?

Anyway, noting the young lady's terrible disappointment, the decision was made to share one of my grandfather's stories with her. He called it "An Old Indian and His Horse." A friend has since provided a similar (handwritten) version of that story (author unknown) under the title, *"Horses In Heaven."* Here is that version:

HORSES IN HEAVEN

An old man was riding his horse down a dirt road with fences on both sides. They came to a gate and looked into what appeared to be a beautiful grassy pasture. That of course was what the old man and his horse were looking for, but a 'no trespassing sign' let it be known that visitors were not welcome.

Then to the gate came a gatekeeper dressed in a dazzling white robe. "Welcome to Heaven," he said. The old man was happy and started to ride his horse in, but the gatekeeper stopped him. "Animals aren't allowed here in heaven. You can enter but he can't come with you."

The old man asked, "What would heaven be without my faithful companion? He's been with me his entire life. If he isn't worthy of heaven, neither am I."

"Suit yourself, old man, but I'll warn you proper— the devil's on the road just ahead. The devil will say anything to sweet talk you into his pasture, but no horses are allowed. You'll both spend your eternity on this hot, dusty road."

The old man looked at his tired, thirsty, and hungry horse and said, "At least we'll be together."

They continued on their way and after awhile they came to a run down fence with a gap in it. No gate— no gatekeeper— just a hole. An individual who seemed to belong there was on the other side of the fence. He asked the old man if he and his horse might wish to come in and rest in the shade— have a drink of water.

"There's a cold water spring under that tree over there and

169

plenty of grass for your horse."

As the old man dismounted, he said, "I was hopin' fer heaven, but they turned me away. They don't allow no animals in heaven."

"Are you talking about that fellow back down the road? That wasn't heaven and he was the devil. The two of you get rested-up and I'll escort you to the front gate." And it was then the old man discovered that he and his horse had been returned to their youth.

If there is a moral to the story of An Old Man and His Horse, it might be from an old proverb:

"Don't respect those who can't respect you."

•••

"Eye has not seen, nor ear heard, nor have entered into the hearts of man those things that God hath prepared for those that love him. But God hath revealed them unto us by his Spirit for the Spirit searcheth all things, yea, the deep things of God." 1
Corinthians 2:9,10

Ask and Receive

Such verses (above) should encourage us to search our souls to determine if we have truly received the *Spirit of* God that enables us to *read between the lines* so that we might know those things that are freely given to us of the spirit. Christ told us our heaven is within us. In other words, much of what we desire and ask of him will be among our eternal blessings. If you wish for your animals to be reunited with you in heaven, ask! Jesus did tell us that our father knows what we need before we ask... but why not ask anyway? "Ask, and you shall receive." That's the bottom line if Jesus was telling the truth, and since Jesus is the truth, he was surely telling the truth.

Mark 9:23 declares that *everything is possible for those who believe.* Therefore, all one has to do in order to be assured of having their animal in heaven is to ask and believe! It is like asking for forgiveness of sins. Seek forgiveness, be truly penitent and believe the sins will be forgiven. Forgiven and forgotten as if those things had never happened. Though the sins be as scarlet, they will be washed white as snow. And after all, when our remorse and inner self-disgust exceeds our act of wrongdoing, isn't that in itself the greatest punishment that could ever be inflicted upon us?

Most religions encourage prayer. Prayer is the child speaking to the Father, but many religions furthermore urge meditation (a form of concentration) wherein the Father can speak to the child. The two:

prayer and meditation, go together like a horse and a buggy, and you really shouldn't have one without the other. Yeah... that was borrowed from the old song, "Love and Marriage," but it's true— so try it. Pray and meditate! The one seeking divine spirituality is only halfway there without meditation.

It has been said that to be merciful without being just is a contradiction. Consider then, Matthew's 18th chapter which says *whatsoever men shall bind on earth shall be bound in heaven...* and that if any two shall agree on what they are asking— that anything they ask shall be done for them in heaven. Do you believe the Bible speaks the truth? Then believe animals go to heaven, for billions will be asking.

"The effectual fervent prayer of a righteous man availeth much."
James 5:16

There are a few of those skeptics who seem to relish engaging in their argument that animals won't go to heaven. They seem to delight in telling animal lovers that nothing in the Bible indicates they will. Do you agree?

Through the years, I have heard so many persons describe their visualizations as to what heaven or hell might be like, that it would be fair to say some of them could turn heaven into hell or hell into heaven. Sam Martin once said that if heaven turned out to be the place a lot of his relatives thought it to be— he'd rather take the alternative flight to the place he would spend his eternity. But to Sam, there were no *alternatives.* Like Will Rogers, wherever the animals were going— that's where he (also) wanted to be.

Ladies and Gentlemen, you are asked to note that the scales are now tipped 100% in favor of the animals. So obvious is the evidence that I wonder if those who still say animals cannot inherit eternal life might be suffering from an attention deficit disorder having to do with a scriptural learning disability. If not, they surely haven't done their homework!

> "It is a foolish thing to make a long prologue
> and be short in the story itself."
> **Maccabees**

The Lamb of God

When John the Baptist first announced Christ, did he say here is the *man* who takes away the sins of the world? No, he said, "Behold the *Lamb* of God which taketh away the sins of the world." Not *man*, but *Lamb*. Get that? Some might think it strange that one of the very symbols for Jesus Christ in Christian liturgy is that of an animal— especially since according to some, an animal is a beast that faces destruction of its very existence at the endtime.

Doubtful the heavenly editors would have allowed such an animal inference to be directed to one who would hold the power of life eternal by comparing him to a creature who was already on the chopping block of annihilation. Remember also the place chosen for the birth of Christ— a manger— an abode of animals.

And there came wise men from the east to Jerusalem, saying
"Where is he that is born King of the Jews, for we have
seen his star in the east and have come to worship him."
"You will find him in a manger wrapped in swaddling clothes."

Would you like to have that run by you once again? Just who [really] was this *stranger in the manger,* and consider the company he was greeted by at his birth— some of those faces that formed his first images of what represented life on earth. According to Martin Luther's, 'Away in a Manger,' the first sounds that Jesus, the Lamb of God heard... and to which he awakened would be the sounds of cattle lowing. The sounds of animals.

174

Bless the Beasts

There is a Christian group known as the Franciscan Order that has encouraged its followers to bring their pets to a place of worship for a special blessing through which they can celebrate what is known as the *Bond of Creation.* This is a time when pets are blessed and sprinkled with holy water. This group was originally founded by St. Francis who at one time stood to inherit a vast fortune and turned it down after having seen a vision of Christ. Thereafter, he assigned himself to a vow of poverty and dedicated his life to the poor and to animals. Even a non-religious person would be hard-pressed to declare that St. Francis was not one of the greatest and most religiously sincere human beings to have ever lived. His single example of wholesomeness should be enough to make many of us hang our heads in shame. Wholesomeness is another word for love.

There are at least 4500 Catholic saints. St. Francis was among the Patron Saints who were chosen for something they had been closely associated with in life. Because Francis loved animals large and small, including bees and butterflies, he became the Patron Saint of Animals. Some also consider him to be the Patron Saint of Science and Ecology. His physical

Ben Garwood

remains have been placed to rest on an altar and some of his original garments hang nearby. There are several blood-curdling stories associated with this man's life— well worth a jaunt to the library.

"Let us be true. Such is the highest maxim of art and life."
Amiel

The Saints Go Marching In

Some of our fellow Protestant friends are now and then amused with what they consider to be our preoccupation with Catholic Saints. Although like some, we don't worship saints— to us every day is sort of an "All Saints Day."

Below our many bird feeders stands a statue of St. Francis, the patron saint of animals, and in one of our gardens, a statute of St. Fiacre, the garden Saint. Say what? Graven images? C'mon now. Our statues are no more graven images than the Presidents on our U.S. currency or Mount Rushmore. And they are not images of God, rather simple reminders of good people, who at least by the end of their lives became determined to leave the world a better place than they found it. If we give ourselves a gentle nudge, God willing, perhaps we could follow in their footsteps?

Is the image of Lincoln on Illinois license plates a graven image? And if there was ever a graven image—wouldn't it be Christ on the cross?

Let's consider asking just what is a saint? The early Christians considered anyone who believed in Christ to be a saint. St. Matthew, St. Mark, St. Luke, and St. John are those we are all familiar with and the ones who lead the list— but all believers were saints to the early Christians.

It was in times to come—later day canonization when the title "Saint" was assigned to a person who had risen above the call of duty. The title then represented an outstanding human accomplishment pertaining to those things considered holy.

So saints weren't always perfect. So what? Does anyone know of a single person who was or is? Jesus said such a person never existed—and included himself in that count. Ambrose Bierce once mused that saints were once sinners who, following death, were reinvented. Again, let's ask, "So what?" What if because of once having been sinners, they repented their former behaviors and became better persons? Wasn't that the entire theme behind Solomon? We should all hope as much for ourselves!

Now Augustine expressed a strong personal reluctance when it came to saints. He found disturbing fault with praising persons to the extent that they became saints. Much of Augustine's resistance probably had to do with earlier pagan practices. Although Augustine's mother was a devout Christian, his father was a pagan. Such inner-marriage was quite common, and the pagans were not the horrifying menaces to society that many persons perceive them to have been. Likely Augustine's feelings simply favored Christ's directive to let the dead bury their dead. Perhaps he felt that when persons departed were made saints, they were all but being kept alive.

Even so, many religions do recognize sainthood, and if for no other reason, it seems to be a worthy custom because it draws attention to exemplary behavior. Is such sacred recognition that different from the secular practices of the military giving medals of honor to soldiers—or the Oscars, the Emmy's, the Pulitzer Prize, or the Nobel Peace

Award? Our society recognizes excellence in many ways.

The earliest Catholic saints were martyrs, then later bishops were eligible to become saints. By the 6th century, "Saint" was being used by the church to honor all champions of Christianity. The list of saints who loved animals and believed animals would be in heaven is impressive and would include Saints Anthony, Francis, Gerasimus, Martin, Thomas, Brigid, ad infinitum.

As St. Francis was said to have preached to the birds, St. Patrick was said to have preached to the wolves, and many are the stories having to do with saints and wolves. Such stories would seem to be shadowed with doubt since the wolves were often considered to be associated with demons, as were cats. But~ the stories are numerous and so similarly told, that it seems certain some saints did number wolves and other beasts of the wild among their closest friends. There is one particularly interesting story about wolves having led some saints to safety through a blinding winter storm.

So when one might see the statue of St. Francis standing in our garden atrium and greeting the birds, they should recognize the fact that he serves only as a friendly reminder that long, long ago, there were other individuals who like ourselves, loved animals.

"Oh Lord, we want to be in that number when the saints go marching in."

Q

What does one call a saint who ends up in hell?

A

Lost.

Shoe On The Other Foot

And as for those who are ready, willing, and able to paint God as a villain who would, without so much as blinking— destroy all animal life, have they not lost sight of "As ye would have others do unto you, do ye also unto them?

What if the shoe were put on the other foot? Would God, if the powers were reversed, wish for the animals to destroy him? You see, it doesn't take a legal eagle or a theological genius to read between the lines of sacred scripture and realize that when it was stated *the Lord giveth and the Lord taketh away,* it wasn't referring to the endtime tenure of his animals. God doesn't destroy that which pleases him.

"And God saw everything he had made and behold, it was very good."
Genesis 1:31

180

Bits, Pieces, Nuts n' Bolts

To the ancient Egyptians, cats were considered gods, and from one era of history to another, animals have been credited with having magical powers. Egyptian leaders were buried with their pets so as to be sure of being with them in the next life. Even the stars were named in Zodiac terminology, meaning *from the circle of animals.* Many ancient astronomers believed star-clusters to be living, super-sized heavenly animals. Even today, everything from athletic teams to automobiles might be named after animals. Animals have long represented man's quest for strength and power... and where might we suppose those notions in man's brain originated? The word zodiac, defines an imaginary belt, within which the planets and the moon travel. At one time, the constellations of the zodiac were given the names of the animals, i.e., lion, goat, scorpion, crab, bull, ram, fishes, etc. Understand that "zodiac" refers to astrologers— not astronomers. *Short History of Astronomy,* Berry.

Whatever the attachments of the past, most modern day pet ownership has to do with companionship— a union between two living entities that have bonded in importance with one another. For at least 12,000 years for dogs and 4,000 years for cats, those two species alone have constituted the domesticated partners of humankind. The relationship between the two is more complex than even the wisest of the wisest among us have ever been able to explain. Such is nothing less than a mutual admiration society. It is not a commitment based on I love you because I need you, but I need you because I love you.

> "Fools give you reasons, wise men never try."
> **From the South Pacific song, Some Enchanted Evening**

However defined, many such a relationship has been proven genuine when one of the twosome willingly sacrificed its life for the other. Jesus said *greater love* has *none* than the one who would lay down life for *another*. Just an hour earlier, this evening's news reported an elderly man was walking his small dog when a vicious Rottweiler attacked. The old fellow placed himself between the two dogs in an effort to save his dog's life. He was badly mauled, but succeeded in keeping the aggressor at arms length by allowing it to take his hand in its mouth. And when it was all over, was he concerned for his own injuries? No. He was just thankful that his "baby" wasn't injured. The last thing he said on the evening news was, "My dog is my whole life. He's everything to me." Hey up there, Mr. God... might you be listening? Of course he's listening! God does not sleep!

Just a week earlier, the evening news told of a young man who defied fire-fighters while running into a burning building to save the life of his trapped dog. He succeeded, and probably couldn't have cared less after being arrested for his gallant and heroic deed.

An Old Woman In A Shoe

There is an old woman who lives in a shoe! Through the profits from our books, Mary and I seek out animal rehabbers in need of financial assistance and we are often overwhelmed with our discoveries! One rehabber whom we now call *The Old Woman Who Lives in a Shoe—* has so many animals she doesn't know what to do. But what she does do is provide them with the same loving care that a human mother would give her children. Nothing less. Her cupboards are not bare, but her cup certainly does not runneth over. Yet she provides dozens of sanitized cages and larger pens where she attends to her orphans in a meticulously clean and disinfected environment. Licensed animal rehabilitators in Illinois are strictly governed by state law and the *Old Woman Who Lives in a Shoe* follows each regulation to the letter. She spares life and gives liberty to thousands of animals that otherwise would surely have perished— some under horrendous conditions.

The *Old Woman Who Lives in a Shoe* is but a single example of such human love and compassion, because the State of Illinois has somewhere near 400 such licensed animal rehabilitators. So it is now asked of those readers in search of truth, will Almighty God

183

after having watched this kind-hearted, altruistic lady, and so many others like her, not give them the only reward they ever hoped for? Will the altruism of any old woman in a shoe who sacrifices countless niceties of life such as color television, a late model car, VCR and other modern conveniences to provide food and medical assistance to needy fur-bearing animals be dishonored by God?

Will they be denied all continuous association with those animals? Does it mean nothing that after their children were raised and gone, they devoted their experienced mothering instincts as surrogate mothers to those of a lesser species in need? There is a proverb from the Plymouth Pulpit that says whatever is sung to the cradle goes all the way to the coffin. Perhaps when these wonderful animal rehabilitators sing to the cradles of their foster children, those melodies will go far beyond the grave.

To those who have ears to hear— God's preview of his love speaks louder than any words to the contrary. God is love. God is love. God is love. Some people just don't seem to hear that. Except for God, could it be that some animal might be the only friend we'll ever have who loves us more than we love ourselves? And how often might we wish we were the worthy person that animal believes us to be?

"Let one go where they will, they can only
find as much beauty or worth as they carry."
Ralph Waldo Emerson

Friends Forever

Not long ago, a very close friend of 35 years was called to his heavenly home. His wife had preceded him in death, and now suffering from heart disease he was involved in the countdown of his final days. His remaining joy in life was his arthritic old dog, "Scrapper." Every day the two friends shared gentle walks and rides in the old Ford pick-up truck to visit his wife's gravesite. At nighttime Butch would sit at his kitchen table and read his Bible to Scrapper, and for hours at a time, faithful old *four-paws* would recline beside him and pay attention as if understanding every word. [It is well known that St. Francis preached to the animals and they are said to have listened intently.]

One evening in late June, Butch heard a crash at the back door. Just as he raised from his chair, three juveniles burst into his kitchen. In his youth, Butch, a highly decorated Korean veteran, could have taken those three punk home-invaders out in a heartbeat, but now he was stiffened from arthritis. So was Scrapper, but during that moment when duty called, Scrapper seemed to forget his disability. What ensued was a flurry of fur and teeth that resulted in all three intruders fleeing, with two of them suffering significant puncture wounds that led to their apprehension.

"You're only a dog, old fellow, and you've had your day;
But never a friend of all my friends has been truer than you alway."
Julian S. Cutler

Just a few nights later, Scrapper suffered a heart attack. Butch immediately dropped to the floor and began giving the dog heart massage while doing his best to blow into his nostrils and mouth. Whether or not Scrapper would have recovered anyway was anyone's guess, but recover he did! Then, a week later, Butch suffered a massive coronary from which he did not survive. He was found the next morning on his kitchen floor— face down with faithful Scrapper laying by his side and whining. If an animal can lament for the loss of its master, would not the Master lament the loss of his animals?

On the very day Butch was buried, his dog followed him in death. Just prior to the moment of his death, Beethoven said his work on earth was now complete. One could not help but wonder if Scrapper similarly knew his mission on earth had been fulfilled. If Butch could have spoken to the dog at that moment, he would have said, "Well done, thou good and faithful servant," but who would not hope that the Lord God Almighty had already delivered that message to both Butch and his dog who are now together again? Butch had rescued that animal from the pound when he was but a puppy, and together they shared the last eleven years of life.

"A faithful friend is a strong defense
and he that hath found one hath found a treasure."
Ecclesiastes

What does a dog and a tree have in common?

A

Their bark.

When the scripture states: "Men and animals are in his care," surely "care" must not pertain only to their physical existence or animals would not be the victims of nature, other animals, hunters, non-vegetarian diets, abusers, or experimental research. Therefore since God is eternal, the scripture is speaking of eternal care.

So once again the question is asked: From whom do we seek answers as to whether animals will inherit eternal life? Beyond all the data to be found in this book, religiously mature readers are strongly encouraged to read *In Search of Truth.* Other than that, perhaps the best reply is to be found from within our own inner-self. Such a search would involve the opening our sixth sense to the enlightenment of the spirit. In so doing we will also tune out that pollution of prejudice-based reasoning that threatens to poison our own spiritual intellect. If we so much as wish to become truly free and independent thinkers— we've already embarked on that task and we can now answer to the higher calling.

"Who loves me will love my dog also."
St. Bernard of Clairvaux

187

Animal Heroes & Heroines

Could *"clever like a fox"* be more than just an expression? Do animals think in logical sequence? Some persons say animals think only according to pre-programmed instincts necessary for survival. How is it then that dogs react to the rattle of car keys, the knock at the door or the sound of a buzzer? How long does it take a dog to respond to the word "cookie" or to identify with the sound of a can opener? Of course animals think! Like humans, they process thoughts according to need. Their imaginings are far from being restricted to natural instincts. But just how well do animals think?

Consider that nearly everyone is knowledgeable having to do with the protection provided by a trained attack dog, but how about untrained rats? Would anyone think a rat would be capable of sensing danger to another being to the extent that it would viciously attack a pair of intended-murderers? No? Perhaps you'd be interested in what Dorothy Huffman has to say in her book, "Heroic Rats." If you said, "No," you stand corrected.

There are countless stories of pets that have awakened their people in the dead of the night to alert them of fires and floods. Recently, one dog even alerted its owner that a falling meteorite was soon to hit the dwelling, and elsewhere a pet raccoon dragged a human baby from a house engulfed in flames. Could animals be the helping hands of guardian angels?

From bears to armadillos, from birds to porcupines, these credible documented stories can be found in abundance. Read how a pot-bellied pig saved the life of a drowning boy in *The Tales of Animal Heroes,* by Allan Zullo. Or go online and click "Animal Heroes" for extensive listings of similar books. Animals do think and animals can reason. Like humans, they vary in intelligence and perception capabilities.

"I agree with Agassiz.
Dogs possess something very much like a conscience."
Charles Darwin

Could such a thing be possible? Perhaps such messiahs have already existed. Before exiting this exploratory manuscript, it is necessary to emphasize the existence of many altruistic individuals who, like Saint Francis, are just that— angels of mercy for the animals. Some are veterinarians, while others are rehabilitators or rescuers. And let's not forget the pet owners and persons without house pets who invest time and money to feed the foraging animals of the wild who come to their homes hoping for handouts. Any such person brings hope to the animals and hope is the message of a Messiah.

"As there is a special place
for all the souls of men according to their number,
so is there also of the beasts."
Enoch LV111-5

Say What?! Say ENOCH

Who, pray tell, is Enoch? It took what seemed like forever, but years ago I read through the entire Book of Enoch. Talk about a spiritual journey! Why don't more Christians read what Enoch had to say? Probably because they've never heard of him! You see, even though Enoch is one of the most important of all the Bible cast, to many Bible readers he's just another name on that long list of who begat whom, ad nauseam. But there's no nausea or boredom when it comes to Enoch!

So Enoch said, after having been taken to that place where no other human was or has since ever been, that there is a *special place* (he didn't say it was heaven) for the animals. What else did I interpret Enoch having to say about animals? He said God will not be judging any animals for the sake of man, but that he would judge human souls for the sake of their animals. Enoch said when the day of judgment comes, that every animal soul will testify against every human soul who wronged it. On that day, all needless lawlessness will be held against that person's own soul. Doing any harm to an animal is an evil transgression. Thus spake Enoch.

Aside from Christ, Enoch might be the most important character of the entire Bible. Let's add to that... he or she who has not observed Enoch and sought additional reference there beyond, has not even scratched the surface in their search for truth.

"They that be wise shall shine bright as the firmament."
Daniel 12:30

Enoch gave confirmation of those spirits waiting to be born and rendered new meaning to God's telling us through the prophets that before we were in the womb, he (God) knew us. Through Enoch, we learn that our soul not only survives bodily death by entering a new dimension, but that our soul originally descended from a house of souls *waiting to be born* and therefore preceded the physical birth of the body. Whatever befalleth man likewise befalleth the animals?

Who but Enoch told us that whatever God turns his face from will cease to be? Does such a statement somewhat confirm we might be living in that hypothetical state of virtual reality... in the mind of God?

"Now we see through a glass, darkly; but then face to face."
1 Corinthians 13:12

So let's put that question up front once again. Could this existence of a prior spirit also have been applicable to animals? Should it not be of at least passing interest to a genuine truth seeker that Enoch was taken by God? Could any true Christian be fulfilled in their spiritual journey without knowing what happened next?

You see, either after or during that experience and his return to earth, Genesis says Enoch was no more but not before he told of his experiences in writing.

Care to have that run past you again? Enoch was no more! Gone. Vanished. Where was he? What does "no more" mean? As for where Enoch went, Genesis simply says God took him. Although maybe not of interest to those persons who believe their spiritual journey to already be complete, Enoch's writings are now available after an absence of nearly two thousand years. Maybe persons who do believe their journey to be complete— rather than to seek the truth, are fleeing the truth? Could that be a whole new bottom line? If Columbo were to be assigned to this missing person file, doubtful he would have smoked another cigar and called it a day? Are you willing to do that?

The rest of the story, in a nutshell, goes like this: Enoch, who incidentally was the grandfather of Noah, was taken by God and given to see the mysteries of the universe and the future of all that is to come. And it's not just Genesis that speaks of Enoch. Enter the New Testament. Christ *quoted* Enoch, so Genesis must have been doing more than spinning wives tales. Hebrews 11, while speaking of faith, in the 5th chapter mentions that Enoch was *translated* that he should not experience death.

In other words, Enoch did not die. Enoch got out of this world alive. But that's just the beginning of the story. The General Epistle of Jude not only makes mention of Enoch, it quotes from the Book of Enoch. It is blather and gibberish talk that suggests the Book of Enoch was derived from a false prophet. Enoch might have been the most reputable Old Testament prophet of all.

> "He that would know what shall be— must consider what has
> been."
> **Eliot 19th c.**

.   As to the exact origin of Enoch's writings... that's still up for grabs. *The Book of Enoch* was known to be in existence centuries prior to Christ, and for some hundreds of years following the resurrection of Christ, "Enoch" was highly regarded by the early church as authentic gospel. And then —it was banned— all known copies were destroyed! That should come as no surprise to those who study Bible history, for such persons know that at one time the mere possession of prohibited scripture or anything that could be read in one's native tongue was cause enough to be sentenced to death.

Was that in fulfillment of Daniel's prophecy that the *words* were to be *closed up and sealed until the end of time*? But yet, it is also written that God's word shall never pass away. Perhaps that is why that following the passing of more than another thousand years and many centuries beyond, the search for "Enoch" became a major focus among Bible scholars. It was not until nearly the 1900's that Enoch's writings were resurrected.

Even many of those who were once the greatest skeptics, cynics, disbelievers and doubting Thomas' are now acknowledging the authenticity of Enoch's writings. There is also that aforementioned evidence that Christ had extensive knowledge dealing with Enoch. So those who would prevent us from knowing the truth banned Enoch temporarily, but not before he revealed that there is a place of eternal abode for the animals.

Everything else in this world can be put on hold —the *things to do list*— but the search for spiritual truth must be <u>now</u>.

What a field trip Enoch's experience would make for science classes. He described the abode of anguish and torment as well as several heavens— paradises desirable beyond human elucidation. And oh boy, did he ever describe hell in living Technicolor! Whoops... my error. He described it in shades of gray.

"We don't just *go to heaven,* we **grow** to heaven."
Edgar Cayce
Edgar Cayce was a spiritual psychic, telepathic clairvoyant... believed to have occult powers.

For This Reason

How can we possibly conclude the answer to this lingering question, "Do animals go to heaven?" Well, for those who have eyes to see and ears to hear, and are capable of being enlightened by the spirit, methinks we already have. But when we do approach the Christian religion as a source to substantiate that answer, we should consider that Jesus said he came to this world not for the whole, but for those who were sick and in need of a physician. Since the animals were not sick by that assumed spiritual definition, why would Christ have taken time from his short visit to detail their eternity? Jesus didn't come here to bring salvation to animals— so there is no reason for scripture that focuses on the mission and objectives of Christ to address that subject any more than extraterrestrial life.

Common sense would suggest that if animals go to heaven, they were already guaranteed salvation— from the very moment of their conception. Beyond that they weren't part of the equation. That possibility of pre-destination certainly sounds reasonable. Should one wish to learn about classic literature, they wouldn't seek such knowledge in an algebra text. The Bible is a human text and since we don't have an animal text, we must read between the lines and allow the spirit to guide us to the hidden truths wherein the answer to our question can be found.

Ever notice how so many people can wag their tongue and say nothing? Then along comes a dog that wags his tail a couple of times and says it all. Someone recently handed me a quote that said no one appreciates your conversational genius so much as a dog. "A, they're Adorable, B, they're so beautiful, C, they're a cradle full of charms! And remember Alexander Pope's quotation in which he said histories are more filled with the fidelity of dogs than of friends?

That's just about it for this book. Books are for learning and hopefully this book offered just that. Could Thomas Jefferson's idea of heaven have included dogs or could it just have been a library? He did say he couldn't live without his books. Alexander Pope said he loved books better than his friends, and some people claim they can't sleep unless surrounded by their books. Suppose books can go to heaven? Emerson once defined a book as being the *eye that sees it all.*

> *"Some books are to be tasted, others to be swallowed,*
> *and some few to be chosen and digested."*
> **Thomas Aquinas**

Common Bonds

If there is anything that many persons do have in common, it is their love of animals. Yet stories abound of those having had friends who had no association with animals and the miraculous changes that entered their lives after experiencing the bonding of just a single animal.

Both Greeks and Early Christians believed animals to have special healing powers. Most of them probably don't think of themselves as such, but animal therapists are in a manner of speaking, faith healers. Animal therapists take trained animals to children's hospitals, care-shelters, education centers and other places where healing and comfort is needed. One might even go so far as to say many a household pet was the trailblazer through which some human souls were able to wing their way to heaven. If that is correct, then why would the Author of all that exists deny the final gift of life-eternal to the animal who assisted in making that blessed possibility a reality for its human soulmate? Consider what Plain Jane had to say about her first spiritual awakening.

"May all that have life be delivered from suffering."
Buddha

197

Cruelty, Inc.

But there are many who do not embrace the encompassing beauty of nature or its creatures. Some members of the human race have always treated animals as nothing less than disposable items. Shocking, but at this very moment, 1000 species of animals are on the brink of becoming extinct. Some of the worst examples of man's inhumanity to those animals that wished for nothing more than to be man's servants and friends can be realized through the study of history. For thousands of years it was the horses that carried men into combat, while other animals shared the burden by carrying the equipment and pulling their wagons. These helpless four legged-beings were thus required to painfully sacrifice their lives along with the warmongers who mounted them or whose chariots they pulled.

In the 4th c. A.D., St. Basil of Caesarea felt the suffering for such animals and remembered them with a prayer: "And for these also, Dear Lord, the humble beasts, who with us bear the burden and heat of the day, and offer their guileless lives for the well-being of their country, we supplicate Thy great tenderness of heart, for Thou has promised us to save both men and beast." St. Basil did believe animals share the afterlife.

Shortly after Mary had written *Pawprints Upon My Heart,* a reader sent her a letter in which she cited a quote by William Ralph Inge: "We have enslaved the rest of the animal creation, and have treated our

198

distant cousins in fur and feathers so badly that beyond doubt, if they were able to formulate a religion, they would depict the Devil in human form."

"Even Satan wouldn't be able to brew up a hell that could compare
to what some men have turned earth into."
Samuel Martin

Without question, the cruelest single example of all times against the animals had to do with the slaughter of tens of thousands of exotic animals that were gathered from all over the world and brought to Rome to die in that amphitheater. Among others, we find elephants, lions, chimpanzees, tigers, crocodiles, hippopotami, lynxes, panthers, bears, boars, wolves, giraffes, ostriches, stags, leopards, antelopes, apes, and rare birds numbered among the innocents. Some were kept in zoological gardens while others were trained to do tricks, but most were forced to fight to the death with one another or men— and 'hunted' for sport in front of the nearly 200,000 roaring fans as they were massacred with clubs, spears, arrows and javelins.

"You serpents, you brood of vipers,
how are you going to escape being sentenced to hell?
Matthew 23:15

In a single day the sacrifice of hundreds of tigers, rhinoceros, hippopotami, elephants, or bears, could have been witnessed by those sadistically sick persons. On the dedication day of the Coliseum, 5000 innocent animals went to their demise from lashings, darts, and hot irons as well as other instruments of death. Condemned criminals as well as men and women consisting of Christians, slaves and sometimes pagans were often cast to starving beasts.

"For I have no pleasure in death, sayeth the Lord."
Ezekiel 33:11 also 18:23,32

Score at the halftime: Lions 12, Christians 0? If salvation was not in the future of those animals and human beings, was this obscene delight of man's desire God's only purpose in having implanted the breath of life within their bodies? Pope Pius V recognized that *for as long as man massacres animals, they will kill each other.* In 1567, Pope Pius V did his best to end all animal fights and other animal torture, but far from being his allies, Pope Innocent VIII, Pope Pius IX, and Pope Paul VI held no value for animals. *The Decline and Fall of the Roman Empire,* Gibbon.

"There must be some way to undo what you done done."
Algonquin J. Calhoun

Construction Zone Ahead

Truth is— probably anyone who does take-up residence in that New Jerusalem will be a person who prior to that day of occupancy had not even a clue of what it would be like. Did even Jesus know? He did say he was going to *prepare* a place for us. Well, for some of us, at least. Could that suggest even though his father's kingdom might already have had many mansions, that the blueprint of our subdivision was not yet complete? Jesus admitted there were those things that neither he nor the angels in heaven knew. Does heaven have rules?

Since Jesus lived with us in our human environment and understood our emotions, would he have tossed a dog a chunk of wood rather than a scrap of meat— and when it comes to heaven, would he do less for you or your animals?

"What man is there of you, whom if his son asks bread, will he give him a stone? Or if he asks for fish, will he give him a serpent? If ye, then, being evil, know how to give good gifts to your children, how much more shall your Father which is in heaven give good things to them that ask him?"
Matthew 7: 9, 10, 11

Jesus first set the example, then taught us to pray without ceasing. He told us that whatsoever was asked in his name would be received. Now whereas it might be true that nearly half of all pet owners do believe that pets or animals in general can go to heaven, rest assured that 100% of those who love animals would be more than twice-warmed if they could know for sure that animals do go to heaven. Most are probably praying for that to happen. Hmm... what if the animal goes to heaven but the person doesn't? What if by "choice" the human doesn't go to heaven?

Countless animal lovers have been willing to take an oath affirming that their heaven would be hell anyway if their animals were not with them, and that they would willingly forfeit their place in heaven if their animals could go in their stead. Is that not even a greater love than one who would lay down his or her life for a friend since such a person would be willing to forfeit their eternity for an animal? A great many persons have said they would do the same for the sinners in hell, believing the life circumstances of those unfortunates and not their premeditated will to do wrong had placed them there.

The scripture below suggests there will be a time of peace when all animals will co-exist in harmony. Of course it doesn't specifically say that place will be heaven, but perhaps Isaiah thought we could put that much together on our own?

"There will come a time when the wolf shall dwell with the lamb
And the leopard shall lie down with the kid and the calf with the
lion."
Isaiah

Love You... Love You Not...

"Whatever befalleth the sons of men befalleth the beasts as they
are all one breath.
A man has no preeminence above a beast,
and he that so reasons is opinionating out of vanity."
Ecclesiastes 3:19

That scripture (above) tells us when it comes to the soul, man has no more rights than the animals. It also assures us that animals and humans cross the same finish line, but there's more beyond that which goes on to say that all go to one place— that place being dust. But it is only the *body* that is returned to dust! Qualified Bible students know that Ecclesiastes represents [Greek] philosophy over prophecy, and like so much scripture, those original words might have long since lost their meaning and be interpreted to mean different things. Although some credit the book of Ecclesiastes to King Solomon, his influence most likely pertained only to the first two chapters of a major compendium of thoughts, and what comes thereafter appears to reflect early Greek viewpoints and attitudes dating back to about the third century B.C.

Few true and independent thinkers believe a loving God would put anyone's eternal soul on the altar of oblivion because they couldn't figure out the *how to get to heaven* perplexities anymore than he would send someone to hell because they didn't understand algebra. As was previously stated, half of the world's inhabitants think all souls will eventually be given the gift of salvation. What about those who were never even given the list of rules— who were subject to being isolated from the "Word?"

It would also be fruitful to recall that such societies as the early Greeks recognized numerous Gods— and if they had that much wrong, how little might some of them have known about anything else? They did the best with what knowledge they had to rely upon.

It is also so important to keep in mind that not every word of the Bible even claims to be divine scripture. It is possible that Ecclesiastes 3:19 could have been written by a student in one of Greek's fine schools for boys. [The girls of Ancient Greece didn't go to schools, rather were educated by their mothers on how to be productive wives.] Therefore, that scripture may have been nothing more than a middle school philosophical term paper. After all, Mozart composed marvelous music at an age when some children would not have yet started school and other societies had their prodigies as well.

Looking just a bit further, we come to Ecclesiastes 3:21. The storm clouds are now gathering, and this is the single scripture upon which most persons who would deny heaven to animals— drop their anchors. "Who knoweth the spirit of man that goeth upward, and the spirit of the beast that goeth downward to the earth?" Notice the question mark the author of those words placed at the end? He is *asking*... admitting he does not know. And does he not confirm it in 3:22

where once again he asks, "...for whom shall bring him (man) to see what is after him?"

So what if the animals don't go to heaven? What if they go downward to the earth? The Jehovah Witnesses believe earth will become their paradise. Perhaps the animals will be here with them and the meek whom scripture says will inherit the earth. If so, rest assured they would surely be well cared for.

Revelations 5:13, speaks of every creature which is in heaven, not both creatures. "Every creature" suggests there are those that might be defined beyond angels and former humans. Perhaps animals? Perhaps advanced incarnations that we have yet to understand?

What self conceited right do we have to assume we are the beginning and the end of God's glory? What if there are hundreds of billions of planets in the universe without end— wherein countless "different" kinds of God's children exist? Ever wonder what God did before he created heaven and earth— or the universe? Read between the lines! There may be more odds and ends out there than ever we could possibly imagine. What if it turns out that even our own souls are subjected to a continuing evolutionary process— becoming more and more pure and expanded— man and animals alike? Victor Hugo described the interior of the soul as being greater than the breadth of the sky.

What "if" we all started out as *bugs*— and what if from there, our consciousness is on a journey that will take us so far beyond the human existence that heaven will be but a rest stop? Maybe there will never be a final ending.

"First find the peace within yourself,
then you can bring peace to others."
Thomas Kempis 4th c.

Let's Wrap It Up

It might be possible to compile a partial list of the many noteworthy persons of the past who did believe animals would go to heaven, but even under the best efforts, that list would still be incomplete. So, let's just add a few more names to those expressing that belief. Although Thomas Aquinas first believed animals could not go to heaven, it appears he was far outnumbered by those who believed they would. St. John Lucas believed animals would go to heaven. St. Paul confidently stated, "Animals will be redeemed." The former Bishop of Salisbury, John Austin Baker, believed animals have souls. Gandhi believed the life of an animal to be no less precious than that of a human being.

And then a miracle. Thomas Aquinas, who once thought animals didn't have souls, changed his mind. He now said that based on scripture, he believed it possible that when Gabriel blows his trumpet on that final day of judgment, animals, who will be in heaven, might even be found testifying for or against humans. Did he secretly keep a copy of the Book of Enoch, or what? Lord Byron, the poet [1788-1824] questioned how any man who in reality is no more than a vain insect himself, could dare to seek heaven's pearly gates while believing animals would be rejected.

Buddha is to be included on anyone's 'Who's Who' list for animals, for he considered that animals and humans alike have *sentient minds that survive death.* Francis of Assisi warned against not including any of

God's animals from the shelter of our compassion. St. Francis of Assisi would have endorsed that statement by Buddha, for he believed everything in the universe is of consciousness and life.

St. Francis loved animals with all his heart. He was probably the foremost animal advocate up to his time who not only believed it was wrong to harm animals, rather declared a higher calling was upon us to service them if they needed our help. After all, any man who would exclude God's creatures from his compassion, said St. Francis, would do likewise to his fellow man. One biography on St. Francis says that *no human tongue could describe the passionate love with which Francis burned for Christ..*

The Holy Father, Saint John Chrysostom, 347-407 A.D., Archbishop of Constantinople, said we must always treat animals with utmost gentleness and consideration, for they are of the same origin as us. John Woolman, 1720-1772. was the Quintessential Quaker, who cautioned against bringing discomfort to any of God's creatures.

"A good deed done to an animal is as meritorious as a good deed done to a human being, while an act of cruelty to an animal is as bad as an act of cruelty to a human being."
Mohammed

We're not finished with that list yet, because on the 18th day of January, 1990, did not one of the most surprising speeches ever made by a Catholic Pope come from the stunning words of John Paul II, when he allowed that animals possess souls and that mankind should treat its animal brethren with love and solidarity? Animals do have souls! To the quickened heartbeats of animal lovers everywhere, John Paul II, like other great spiritual leaders before him, went on to say that animals have within them the breath of life that comes from God.

St. Basil of Caesarea, circa 370 A.D., certainly believed in the afterlife of animals and frequently included them in his prayers. He reminded persons that God had promised to save both men and animals to eternity. St. Paul believed animals would receive the same expectation having to do with deliverance as would any good Christian. There are many religions that make every effort to take a stand for the animals. Take for example, Rabbi Chaim Dovid Haley, who in 1992 issued a rabbinical ruling against making or wearing garments of fur. Such a practice is against the teachings of the Talmud and the Torah.

Nostradamus certainly believed that animals go to heaven. Following the death of his beloved dog, Mystic, he said: *"Is not the source of goodness and reason, God?"* He was expressing his faith that his animal friend was safe in the hands of God.

"The creation itself will be liberated from its bondage."
Romans 8:21

And what says Mary? After all, she was the one who originally conferred the sense of urgency to assist with the answer to the question that has now been addressed. And she is one to whom many animal lovers look to for inspiration and guidance. So what does Mary have to say about whether animals

209

are in heaven? "Without a doubt! Animals not only have a soul, they have a spirit capable of giving and receiving love."

And what about you Amanda? Has this book brought any peace to your mind having to do with whether you will see your departed animal companions again? It is certainly hoped so. Beyond that, we have now had the opportunity to realize that persons of multiple languages and of many belief systems believe that whatever mercy is forthcoming for mankind will be likewise forthcoming for the animals. And let's face it, except by faith, enlightenment by the spirit and the use of our own intellect, we really couldn't prove there is a heaven for humans, so animals have just as good a chance as we do if we have faith for them. If there is a heaven, and surely there is, animals will be there!

Should you still have doubts, realize that doubting is a natural emotion. There was one man who once refused to believe that Jesus Christ had been resurrected. His name was Thomas, and he was one of the chosen twelve. He heard Christ say that he would demonstrate his power to overcome death by rising on the third day, and yet Thomas didn't believe it. Talk about rubbing salt into the wound! So for those who still might doubt animals will go to heaven, let's offer them the same consideration afforded to Thomas for his disbelief. Some people never get the message. Fact is— if the other disciples believed Christ would have returned in three days, wouldn't they have been waiting outside his tomb with some kind of party balloons and colored graffiti?

Animals love and animals love to be loved. Animals share joy and companionship. They rejoice and they mourn. Animals are beings with souls. Animals have eternal life. Such is the consensus of the greatest religious opinions in written history.

One final thought. The story goes that when a man once asked Einstein if he could prove there was a God— Einstein quipped, "Can you prove there isn't? So if someone asks you if you can prove animals go to heaven, you simply reply, "Can you prove they don't?" Einstein added that the deep emotional conviction of the presence of a superior reasoning power, which is revealed in the incomprehensible universe, forms his idea of God.

"God hangs the greatest weights on the smallest wires."
Sir Francis Bacon
"Then ask the beasts and they will teach you... likewise the fowls of the air, for they can also tell you. You can even speak to the fishes of the sea, who will declare unto thee that in God's hand is the soul of every living thing"
Job 2:7-10
"We are truly one soul, for there is nothing but God. The essence of
the soul, being a part of God, is the same in us all— animal, human,
and all sentient life, but each soul is unique, personalized and individualized by our many life experiences. The choices we make
determine our spiritual development and where we will go when we
leave this place."
Vernon Mink

Need anyone say more? No. <u>That</u> says it all.

Better have your leash ready. Surely he comes quickly.
"A righteous man regardeth the life of his beast: but the tender mercies of the wicked are cruel."
Proverbs 12:10
"In the hand of God is the soul of all living things."
Job 12:10
"There is not an animal on the earth nor a flying creature on two wings that they are not people unto you."
Koran
"Beyond the shadow of a doubt,
animals have the same living souls as man."
Buckner
"Not just mankind, but every creature that cometh from God is awaiting eternal life."
Paul's Epistle to the Romans
"Every beast of the forest is mine, and the cattle upon a thousand hills.
I know all the fowls of the mountains,
and the wild beasts of the field are mine."
Psalms 50:10,11
"And I saw heaven opened, and behold a white horse...."
Revelation 19:2
"A man has no preeminence above a beast,
and he that so reasons is opinionating out of vanity."
Ecclesiastes 3:19

The buck stops here:
"As there is a special place for all the souls of men according to their number, so is there also for the beasts."
Enoch LV111-5
"Woof, baa, moo, ribbit, hee-haw..."

MEOW!

(The End)

READ OTHER BOOKS BY BEN GARWOOD:

IN SEARCH OF TRUTH

For those persons who would like to continue their Search for Truth having to do with animal spirituality, read: *In SEARCH of TRUTH.* Some of the subject material found in that book is also contained in this text, however *ANIMALS IN HEAVEN* is a *family oriented book* while In SEARCH of TRUTH is recommended for religiously mature readers only. The contents of that book include:

Mention of the *other* gospels and Christian books, found hidden for centuries, that many Christians have never heard about; glimpses of Bible origins; what ancient scholars, i.e. philosophers, writers, religious leaders, et al, believed having to do with animal spirituality; the insensitivity of the "Lords" over the "serfs" and the denial of women by the church.

In Search of Truth muses Mark Twain's question— that wouldn't having all the fools in town on one's side be a large enough majority for anyone? After all, the early church not only believed in— they executed millions of women as witches; they didn't believe women had souls or for that matter were even human beings.

There is a much deeper inquiry having to do with both human and animal souls. Subjects such as reincarnation, purgatory, and the belief systems of several religions other than Christianity are considered. There is a very close look having to do with the societies of times past and what the brief and often miserable human lifespan was like during the dark and middle-ages.

The philosophies of such men as Voltaire, DesCartes, Aristotle, and others are shared as well as the most positive answer to the question, "Did Christ Live?" (Yes, he did, but the "proof positive" is not in the Bible.) Every Christian needs to know the whole story surrounding the reality of Jesus Christ.

A nearly microscopic look at the early church is found within those pages including some of the leaders of the later church such as Martin Luther, John Calvin, John Wesley, Jonathon

213

Ben Garwood

Edwards, and others. Is our existence and endtime pre-
determined? Did God or Satan create sin? Are we living in a
state of virtual reality? Does nothing really exist except in the
mind of God? Are those Christians who believe only those who
find salvation to be the ones who inherit eternal life, correct?
You'll be interested to hear what some often overlooked
scriptures have to say about that!

There is also a section having to do with angels. Do you have
a guardian angel? Read what the most expert of experts have to
say about angels and perhaps you'll be able to get that good
night's sleep you've been looking forward to but can't seem to
find.

One of this author's oldest friends— a friend of his mothers--
expressed her fear in reading this book, saying it might shake
her faith. Good grief, Gertrude! This book is not about shaking
one's faith— it's about solidifying it— setting it in cement. Jesus
said, "Seek and ye shall find." Others have now done that
seeking. They have experienced the journey and wish to share
their voyage of love and truth with you. Eighty percent of all
Americans now claim to have personally experienced God's
presence. Perhaps by working together and seeking the truth,
we can make that 100%?

GLORY BOUND

Soon to be released, a masterpiece, a *magnum opus* that
required forty years to bring to completion—a dramaturgical
narrative based on the authentic story of an Appalachian
mountain hill preacher who was closely akin to the
denominational circuit riders of the pre and post-Civil War era.
The backwoods folk knew him only as Preacher Bill— this
doctor/veterinarian gospel man who was sometime seen with a
Bible in one hand and a Colt .44 revolver in the other. Little else
was known about him, but he had become a symbol of
righteousness and hope for those who called the mountains—
home.

Time was, before they knew him, this man once resided in
economic splendor. His early life had been one of social
prominence and his intended profession for which he had

received the finest of preparatory education was to become that of a New York physician. Then the angel of death came calling and claimed the only romantic interest of his life.

Shortly thereafter, like a demon released from hell, the Civil War raised its ugly head. Following four years of horrendous experiences as first a horse doctor and then a surgeon for the Union Army, came another calling— an experience so moving that the recipient committed the remainder of his life to becoming a godly physician of the soul. From those moments on, his only mission was to attend the spiritually crippled, the economically maimed, the religiously mangled and the idealistically mutilated that sought refuge by following either their dreams or their tears to a place that some were sure even the angels feared to tread.

Glory Bound is one of the greatest stories ever told— a lifetime of events that will draw smiles and chuckles from the somber and solemn, and yet bring even the most calloused reader to tears. For any person who might feel left behind in today's fast paced world and distraught by the inconsistent trends of present moral philosophies, Glory Bound is spiritually enlightening whether the reader is fundamentally religious, conservative, secular, or undecided. While it has to do with personal spiritual identification, there is no proselytizing or denominational promulgating.

Glory Bound is a compendium of real life action-packed adventures and light-hearted history. This emotionally absorbing narrative of those times all but forgotten will offer strong appeal to environmentalists, animal lovers, and outdoor devotees— including persons who seek inward enlargement of their own spiritual pilgrimage. Whether the reader expects a motivational content having to do with family values and philosophy, or simply thrills and chills... Glory Bound *speaks louder than thunder to all.*

Soon to be released by Tarbutton Press, Glory Bound is an opportunity to climb those magnificent Appalachian Mountains and experience the warmth of glorious mountain laurels, the splendor of beautiful blossoming dogwood trees, and icy trickles of winding mountain streams that turn into roaring rapids. Stories of the captivating and unimaginable personalities of curious and exceptional mountain animals will make each reader want to reach out and stroke their soft, furry coats.

The glitter of gold, the excitement of the Western frontier towns, the Plains Indians and the cattle drives brought legions of curiosity seeking reporters westward to tell *that* story. Had the Wild West never occurred, America's early 19th century interests would no doubt have turned to the intriguing life stories of those human beings snuggled deep in the mountain valleys and hollers to the pinnacles of the summits that towered above. Here was a way of life that few knew existed— a world unto itself that was shrouded by a breathtaking blue haze hovering in mystical-like suspension over the peaks of that great and mysterious range of super hills known as the Appalachian Mountains.

Beyond all this exquisite loveliness is the story of ancient vestiges—an abode of nature that once provided haven for American Indians and tombs for fossilized relics. Here were the remnants of a hundred million years now embraced by the deciduous and coniferous forests where first the animals and then God's children found habitat, shelter, and food.

THE BEGGAR MAN

This 2004 release which will appear in standard print, Braille, and a talking book, is the true story of the author's own grandfather, a blind man born during the Civil War who traveled (alone) by train and coach to more than thirty states during his lifetime. At first, this educated and accomplished musician placed a tin cup in front of him as he sat on wooden boardwalks playing his fiddle and accordion— often offering short sermons while encouraging those nearby to drop a coin into his can. Then one church after another became aware of his musical genius and his oratory skills, and asked if he would assist them with revivals. By the latter years of his life, this father of eleven children had become a much sought-after evangelical revivalist of churches throughout the Midwest. A religious fundamentalist, he was often at Biblical odds with his own family and others during those times when more liberal attitudes were being accepted by most major denominations. Yet the invitations for his very fundamentalist guest sermons as well as his music which included accordion, violin, piano, and organ were many.

For early release copies contact:
Tarbutton Press at 951 Snug Harbor St.
Salinas, CA 93906or email: info@tarbuttonpress.com

217

Printed in the United States
19792LVS00002B/175-198